In Tangier
We Killed the
Blue Parrot

IN TANGIER
WE KILLED THE
BLUE PARROT

BARBARA ADAIR

First published by Jacana in 2004
This edition published by Modjaji Books in 2020
Cape Town, South Africa
www.modjajibooks.co.za
© Barbara Adair
Barbara Adair has asserted her right to be
identified as the author of this work.

Edited by Lionel Abrahams
Cover text and artwork by Jesse Breytenbach
Book layout by Andy Thesen
Set in Palatino

ISBN print: 978-1-928433-08-8
ISBN ebook: 978-1-928433-09-5

PREFACE

It is 11 January 1993 and I am sitting in the Café Hafa in Tangier. The café is about a ten minute walk from the Forbes museum. It is beautiful. If I strain my eyes I can see the sea, the Straits of Gibraltar. My travelling companions have abandoned me, they are visiting something somewhere else in the city, and they want to move on soon.

It feels strange to be sitting in a café in Tangier. For years South Africans have been unable to travel to other countries in Africa. Now, for the first time, with the announcement of the release of political prisoners and the unbanning of the African National Congress, we can travel. I welcome political change in my country, I am hopeful. And I am happy to be able to travel to places that I have never been allowed to go to before.

Morocco is filled with hustlers. Hustles of all kinds, they hustle you for sex, they hustle you for drugs; there is nothing that escapes the hustle. Sometimes it intrigues me, a hustler, does he sell his soul? At other times it is an irritation, like a fly buzzing around my head that I have to flick away.

Today a young boy approaches me; he can't be more than fourteen years old. I try to flick him away but he is persistent. His voice is soft. He has a slight American accent; it is not the heavily accented English of most Moroccans. For a moment I wonder where he learned to speak my language. For an instant I listen to him.

"Look over there," he says pulling at the sleeve of my jacket, "see that old man there, that's Paul Bowles, the famous American writer, see, that's Paul Bowles." I look to where he points. On the other side of the café at a table on the edge of the shaded terraced garden, in the shadow of the overarching blue sky, sits an old man. He has white hair, an aquiline nose and he is writing in a notebook. He does not look up as I stare at him.

The old man with the white hair continues writing. As I leave he lifts up his head and looks out across the sea.

Barbara Adair
11 January 1993

As flies to wanton boys are we to th' gods
they kill us for their sport

King Lear (Act IV, Scene I, lines 36 to 37)
by William Shakespeare

I

Belquassim leaned forward and took a sip from the glass he held in his right hand. He did not usually drink alcohol, which was prohibited to him. But on this occasion, recalling events that had long passed, he needed to drink from a cup of fierce fiery yellow liquid. He raised the glass, To Paul and Jane, he whispered to himself. Strange … he thought. Memories are remembered so that the adventure can be told. The telling of a memory makes the story, the story that is more exotic than the experience. What happened itself is not real, only the story is real. The real adventure. And it can never be repeated. And he had never told this story before.

From further down the bar a woman laughed. The bar was in the Hotel Mirador. In room 35 there was a painting on the wall over the bed. The story was that Matisse had painted it when he was visiting Tangier with Madame Matisse, before he was famous. Belquassim remembered how the hotel employees were always quick to tell anyone who looked like a tourist that Henri Matisse and his wife and, of course, Gertrude and Alice, had stayed in the Hotel Mirador. And, for a small fee, guests could go into the room and look at the painting. For a somewhat larger fee guests could sleep the night under the colours of this revered artist. But really – and Belquassim knew this because he had been into room 35 and Paul had shown him some photographs of the now famous artist's work – the wall just had a few different colours added to it by the painter. A few colours added to the stains of the rust and the damp. Matisse must have been thinking of other things as he splashed his paint across the wall above the bed. Who could tell now? Belquassim wondered if the colours were still there, or if they had been painted over by the new hotel proprietor, who did not know of Matisse, and was unaware of how the history of art had pervaded the walls of the Hotel Mirador. Belquassim wondered if the proprietor had painted the wall a bright white to show how clean it was.

Paul had taught him everything about Matisse and the Parisian painters, he reflected. What had he said? "They tried to express their unconscious desires on canvas. The unconscious is like a Cubist painting. It has no discernible pattern. Straight lines, but they are not linear." Paul also said, "And Gertrude ... She loved collecting the new Paris art. She accumulated sentences and she made art." What had Paul meant by this? How could she collect sentences? Sentences could not be held in a hand, touched, caressed. But he remembered Paul saying that he caressed sentences. Belquassim would watch him when he held a pen. What did he mean? Belquassim remembered Paul's pale white beautiful face and his cold blue eyes, and his voice, soft and gentle and menacing. Everything that he knew had come from Paul: the world, music, poetry, philosophy and love.

Behind the bar were rows of bottles on shelves. Behind the bottles was a painted picture. Blue-headed Touaregs on camels racing through the desert. A tourist picture. A picture those tourists drew of Morocco. Fierce-faced camel riders dressed in blue. The bar was dark. The bottles on the shelves and the stained picture behind them were lit up by a single bare globe. The picture could barely be seen, just as no Touaregs could be seen in Tangier. It was as if it was night. But if Belquassim turned on his stool and looked across the shadowy room he could see the beach. Bright hard sunlight flickered over the long palm fronds that persistently blurred his view. He could see Madame Porte's famous *salon de thé*, it was at the edge of the beach, its red awnings moving in the breeze that blew in from the blue sea. The windows of the salon were closed, Madame Porte was no longer there. He wondered where she was. A seagull stood on the narrow wall that separated the salon from the beach. Its yellow feet clutched the wall, but it could not find a grip, these feet were not made for hard brickwork, they were webbed, meant for water, not walls. It swooped down into the waveless sea and then emerged again. Belquassim could see the shape of a fish in its beak. The curved sharp end plunged into the flesh of the fish. The fish was dead but Belquassim thought he could feel its pain. He could feel that beak slash through his flesh, damaging him, tearing him apart.

Belquassim remembered the long hours in this bar. He remembered the tea in the salon. In these two places he would sit for hours listening to the chatter of the expatriates, the writers and the philosophers. He had learned a lot; a lot about despair and love and hatred, the wars in Europe, the quality of the hashish and opium that could be found in the city. Nothing had changed but the faces, and Madame Porte was gone now. Belquassim walked over to the window of the bar, it was smudged by the salty spray of the sea. He peered out and looked carefully across the water. On a fine day he knew that he could see the coast of Spain. He had never been to Spain. But he knew about the Spanish writer Cervantes. Paul had read extracts from this thick book to him in the evenings as they sat on the veranda of the house. The faithful and foolish Sancho Panza, who loved his master more than he loved himself. Don Quixote, the knight errant, the adventurer. The giants who were windmills. The dream of Dulcinea. Belquassim had never been outside Morocco, although sometimes he believed that he had travelled the world. Travelled through the stories told to him by Paul. Morocco was the world for him then, as it was now. A different world now, but the world anyway. He narrowed his eyes and looked out of the window again. If he looked hard enough maybe he would see Jane's grave in Malaga. A grave without a headstone and without an inscription.

Belquassim walked back to the bar and sat down. He leaned backwards on the barstool. A grave and this tacky bar, he thought. But – he bent his head towards the glass that he drank from – it is not like the bar of the old days in Tangier. The days when Tangier was still part of the International Zone. The old bars smelled of musk and opium, they had the odour of opulence, they reeked of the expatriates. If you sat in a bar for just five minutes you could hear a million languages, dream languages from far away; America. Now the space of the half-day seemed to reverberate with the loneliness that he felt inside him. It reverberated with the woman's laugh. The faded sepia photographs lined through with smoke on the walls were all that was left of that world. The woman smiled at him. White teeth stained with nicotine and red lipstick. For a moment he thought she seemed interested in him, but then she turned to her companion and laughed again. Her purple shirt stuck to her flat chest. The sweat of the city whitened her body. She reminded him of Jane, half-drunk, half-lovely. He wondered what he would do if she came over to him. He could not touch her as he had touched Jane. He could not brush her hair. It would not be the same. He could remember Jane's skin, soft and milky, a girl's skin. Sometimes on that white would appear a dimpled rash, pink spots marring the thin skin. The music from the radio echoed outside his head as he watched the woman get up; slowly she moved her thin body and started to beat time with her shoes. Time seems to have gone so quickly, he thought. And what was this music? Had he heard it before? Maybe, but that was long ago. It sounded like the music that Paul had searched for in the mountains. Unrecorded Moroccan sounds. Now they played it on the radio.

Belquassim tried not to be angry. "Anger," Paul had said, "like jealousy, is a wasted emotion. It takes a person nowhere. It is a waste of time and energy that could be spent differently. If you are angry it means that you care. And I have never cared enough to become angry." Belquassim remembered Paul looking at him with his blue eyes as he spoke these words. "Maybe I do care," Paul continued, "I think I may care a little about beauty. But even that, if it were not here for me to look at I could not get angry. I will just describe beauty in my words if this happens." And even though Belquassim tried not to feel anger, and not to feel jealousy, he could not suppress it. Anger and jealousy, a waste of time and energy. They showed that he cared. And he had nothing else to do with his time or energy. He continued to feel. But Paul was right, it was of no use; he could feel anger and he could feel jealousy until it burst inside his head. Exploded like an orange smashed against the concrete beachfront pathway. The juice shooting upwards into the air. The segments scattering. And then things would be just the same again. People would walk over the orange segments without even seeing them. And things had felt just the same for a long time now.

Belquassim was thirty-five. He had lived his whole life in Tangier. He could remember the incipient stages of the writers' and artists' movement. He had seen the quixotic idealism of the transient residents, their decadence; their drugs and their loves grow up around him. How he loved that life. He loved the lack of morality, he loved the abandonment and he loved to watch. He had watched from the sidelines mostly, or at least until he had met Paul. He saw how people reached out and took whatever they could to pleasure themselves. He loved being an object of that love and that pleasure. It had seemed to him that whatever they, the expatriates, did, they could change the world. But now he knew that they had not changed the world, they had only changed his world.

Paul and Jane had changed his world as they had changed their own world. They had freed themselves from the slow decay of social bondage. Freed themselves from prejudice, tyranny and despair. And yet where were they now?

After meeting Paul and his wife, Jane, Belquassim had begun to believe that even he and his world mattered and had meaning, and that he could belong in the life they showed him. Even he could be free. This was a world that was open to everyone. But those doors had closed now. A world open to everyone, but not any more. He had come so close to living a dream, this world and this life. He could touch it. He could feel it. He could smell it. And Paul had fostered his belief. He was in the constant presence of a dream. He remembered Paul saying, "A writer – for I am a writer now – does not try to escape from reality, he tries to change it so that he can escape from the limits of reality. Don't credit me with this observation," he had added. "It comes from Bill. And Bill has no reality. He has changed it, in his work and in the way he lives." And Belquassim had escaped the limits, he had pushed the limits, and for a short time it seemed as if he had won. They had all escaped. But now, bound by his life he knew that that long sleep was over. The dream was over. He was awake now.

Belquassim remembered that Paul told him about Europe, about America, about a life that seemed so far away from the sun-bleached houses that overlooked the sea in Tangier. He remembered little of what these stories were about, he just remembered wanting to go to these faraway places. He remembered Paul promising to show him the high-rise buildings of New York City. And in return Belquassim told Paul about his country. Stories of his family, the stories his grandfather used to tell him about the caravans that sped across the desert, the hard leather of the bags tied to the sides of the camels loaded with silver and spices. Cracked Bedouin hands. Eyes that could see very little because of the hard sand that blew. The tracks across the desert that only one who has been there before can follow; scars across the landscape. The smell of the Hamatan – but even this hot wind that blows up the dust cannot erase the scars of the wounded. Pictures of the donkey caravan, in the sand the tiny hoofprints, moving in one direction, a donkey highway. Heavy slabs of salt taken from the salt pans. The endless journeys across so much space. Belquassim remembered how Paul loved these stories. From this he would fashion his own tales, tales of intrigue and passion. One world enjoined with another.

Paul had arrived in Tangier early. A long time before most of the other expatriates arrived. His wife, Jane, only came to the city later. Jane was a dark slight woman who appeared to be quite flighty. Paul said that she was not really flighty, she was as gifted an artist as he was, but she had somehow become stuck. Perhaps she had become stuck because of too much pleasure, Belquassim used to think. But now he knew that taking pleasure was the way in which she could become brave. She tried to define herself in pleasure. It was the way that she kept herself safe from those she most loved. How she kept safe from an outside world that she believed sought to judge her. Jane spent most of her time, when she was in Tangier, in the *souks*, constantly exploring another way, her lame leg stiff and unbending. She walked with a limp, unable to bend her right knee. Belquassim would watch her as she walked down the stairs of the house. Her left shoulder would fall downwards as she picked up her right leg and placed it carefully on the next step.

He remembered the story she had told him, the story of how her knee became stiff. "When I was a child," she said, "I became very ill, some sort of wasting disease. My whole body collapsed, it was limp, as if I had no bones. I was like a jellyfish. And when I became well again my right leg was bent and could no longer move." And then she laughed. He remembered the expression on her face when she told him how her mother had taken her to a doctor and how the doctor had straightened her leg. Her words lingered next to him. "All I remember is that I knew that I was vulnerable. You know how we all think that we are vulnerable, but we never think that this is real. It is a sort of contradiction: vulnerable but invulnerable. But after my leg that feeling of invulnerability disappeared. I was no longer brave. I knew that things could happen. I sort of often think about it. The before and the after. The brave me and the cowardly me."

Jane had even learnt how to speak Moghrebi. She had persuaded herself that she was in love with a woman who sold herbs and other medicines in the market. Her name was Cherifa. Cherifa, tall, heavy and dark. She would cover herself with a *djellaba* and *haik* during the day. At home, in the evenings, she would wear a white cotton shirt and faded blue jeans. Her long brown fingers that she used to sift the millet, the long dark fingers that took Jane in the night. Belquassim imagined how they penetrated Jane's body, a knife through her thin chest, a chest that would not be hard to pierce. Cherifa, an old woman now, still sat in the same place in the market, surrounded by young girls. Still sifting the millet with her fingers. Still using the same fingers in the black nights. Cherifa had wished that Jane would die, and that had come true. Was the die cast by her spells?

Jane was so fragile, so indulgent and so stoned, it seemed as if she could die at any moment. Cherifa wanted Jane to die, or so he was told. Cherifa wanted the house that she sometimes lived in with Jane. Belquassim had seen some of the talismans that Cherifa had given Jane, talismans made by sorcerers. The necklace made of the parrot feathers that Jane had hung on a leather cord and which she sometimes wore around her neck. Yellow and green feathers fluttering on her chest bones. The piece of cloth stolen from the sacred tomb of one of the saints, he could not remember which one. She had kept this material next to her bed, next to the first edition of Paul's book. A dirty piece of brown cloth that was sacred and dangerous. He remembered the inscription that Paul had written on the front page of the book, *"To Jane. P.B."*

Belquassim remembered Jane. He had not wanted her to die, and to die so far away from what she loved.

"I met you just in time," Paul often said. "Just in time for my writing to settle. Just in time for me to see the words, to love the words." And the words were all that Paul loved. Paul had found him just in time, Belquassim liked that line. He had liked it because it gave him a sense that Paul needed him, needed him, if not for his love, then at least as an inspiration. Belquassim enabled Paul to write, he had thought that he gave Paul all his ideas, but all he had given him was his name. And Paul was still a writer, he still wrote words now. He remembered exactly when Paul had told him that he needed him. It was a Monday, in 1949. They were both walking out of the house where he and Belquassim, and sometimes Jane and dark haired Cherifa, lived. The house was right in the middle of the winding streets of the old dissolute part of the city, a part of the city that tourists rarely visited. The house near the *Petit Socco*. On that day Paul had been unable to find his way through the streets to the Café Hafa, his favourite café that overlooked the city and the beach. Belquassim had to show him where to go, which streets to follow, what to look out for along the way. He liked this feeling. He liked to show Paul where to go. Just as he liked to tell Paul his stories, just as he liked to listen. He thought he was indispensable.

Paul had come to Tangier to write music and to tape the indigenous music of the country, but he had ended up writing books and stories. Belquassim remembered Paul playing him some of the music that he had written for an opera. The story of a city and a life in it. A story that was written by a friend of his. He wrote music for his friends. As Belquassim sat in the study of the house where the gramophone was he remembered that he could hear in the record the perfumed explosion of the trumpet, that perfect explosion of pain. The pain that he now knew was his relationship with Paul. Pain so beautiful, the pain that his body wanted so much. The needle would hiss over the vinyl, scratching the black skin. Paul's music set out a story that could not be described in words, it could never be told. But even though Belquassim loved the music more than the stories, he knew that Paul needed his words. His stories were like pictures created by hashish, they painted him into an unknown world of raw emotion that he had never recognised or known existed. Only his characters knew of this emotion, but even they were unable to recognise it. And Paul, he thought, wrote better than Jane did. Her stories were always filled with hope, whereas Paul's words were richer, darker, evil. Paul would often say, "I write about space, emotional space, and the desert, with its cold dust and careless sun. The desert," Paul had continued, "was just the right image for this emotional space. The vacuum of humanness, the depletion of anything that resembled meaning or morality. The desert has no rules." Belquassim had not thought so then, but he had not contradicted Paul. He still did not think so. The desert, for him, captured an emptiness that was full of something other than that which was human. It had no human values. It represented a meaning that could not be duplicated or identified in people. Maybe it was God, so vast, so unconquerable, and yet so beautiful. The desert had no man-made rules. It had no rules imposed on it, but had created its own rules. Rules made of nothing but the sun and the sand. Rules that meant a lot.

He looked out again through the long-fronted windows that were open to the ground. The outer humid sea air crept sluggishly up and into him. It seemed to dissipate his anger. Remembering brought him some comfort. The comfort of being older, no longer the in-love and loved young boy, but the older man, angry and jealous, but with an inner recognition of this condition. Suffering, he thought, is just about being alive. The immediacy of my own suffering, maybe, helps me to see the world more clearly. If I know about pain then at least I can know the pain of others. Maybe it will allow me to forgive more easily as I will know that everyone else suffers in much the same way as I do. Maybe this is what he had tried to explain to Paul about the desert. It enabled you to see, it enabled you to thirst for something more, but to forgive those who could not give it to you. But Paul had only been able to see what he wanted to see, everything else remained outside him, cold and distant, dark and unforgiving. Yet Belquassim knew that he had chosen this dark and unforgiving man. He could have walked on, he could have left him after the first night. But instead he had chosen to follow him, and it was the fact that he followed Paul that made him feel alive, the pain of life.

II

Belquassim had met Paul in the bar in the Hotel Mirador. Belquassim used to go there to watch the people, and for the money that he could easily earn. For him what he did was no different from what any woman did in a brothel. It was work. What he did was not always gratifying, sometimes it was shameful, sometimes erotic, but always what he did made him feel somehow richer than those around him. He could not describe why it made him feel rich, he could only say that his experiences gave him more life, more life than that which was handed out to those who placed a brick upon a brick. He smelled life in the sweat and semen of the white men. He could see further than others who were also poor and had nothing. He could see beyond the cliffs that lined the beach, he could see another world, the world outside Tangier. He could even see Spain if the weather was clear.

Belquassim was a thin pretty boy. He practised a languid look. He would watch his eyes in the small mirror that his sister had brought home from the market. She used the mirror to paint her eyes. He also painted his eyes with kohl: a thin black line underneath his lower eyelashes; and if he wanted to he would paint the upper edges of his eyelids. This made him look beguiling, as if he had spent too much time staring at the sun. His pupils became round, dark holes that reflected the light. It gave him an insouciant look, a look that was careless of his real feelings. And his real feelings – sometimes he did not even know what they were: feelings of hunger and want and need, hunger for knowledge, the need to be held close, next to a body, next to skin, the feel of flesh? He knew that he was pretty, this was his advantage over the other boys who mostly looked all the same. Thin and brown and vacant. He thought he was thin and brown and full, full of clever stories, even English stories. This is what Paul said he liked about him. But more than this, Paul liked his questions, he liked it that Belquassim grasped everything that he told him with ferocity, as if he was starved. Maybe he was starved, and his hunger was what was so attractive. Belquassim also did not embrace the ravages of Europe and America as Paul and his expatriate companions seemed to do. Probably because he had never seen the sewers and underground dungeons that served as a railway system, probably as he had never experienced the horrors of self-inflicted destruction. His wars came from outside. And he could never embrace these wars, because he did not want to remember them, so he embraced Paul instead. Embraced a hot body. Paul liked the way Belquassim responded when he read to him; he also liked the soft hairless golden skin of Belquassim's flat stomach and the way in which his circumcised cock would rub against him as they lay close together in the airless damp top room of the house.

In the bars of Tangier the patrons were mostly expatriates; very few Moroccans, unless they were boys like Belquassim, would go into them. This was because few Moroccans drank the alcohol that was served in such quantity. The Muslim code is clear, alcohol is forbidden. And so the Tangier residents who were Moroccan would congregate in the market cafés, where they drank sweet peppermint tea and smoked hashish. But more than the prohibited alcohol – they did not go into the bars because, as a Moroccan, if you went into the bars it meant one thing: you and Faust, the same pact, the inevitable consequences. The bar was the line that separated one world from another. Belquassim did not think this. It was true that he had first gone to the bar at the Hotel Mirador to earn some money. His younger sister was ill, she had the illness of poverty and the illness that was the product of the squalid streets of Tangier. When she coughed she would hold a piece of cotton cloth against her lips. When she took it away mixed in with the outline of her lips and the bile was blood, thin streaks of pink liquid in the grey white cloth, pink embroidery, pretty pink embroidery. Belquassim had earned enough money to take her to the Nazarene hospital where the silent nuns looked after the dying. They put her in a bed with clean sheets on it and they gave her many pills. But it was too late, there was nothing the nuns in their long white habits and black head cloths could do for her, she had died anyway. She had died in the white hospital far away from her home and from those she loved. She had died with the women who loved only Christ.

And then Belquassim had met Paul. And from a voice, from Paul's voice, Belquassim had learnt how to change his world. His sister who had given her life to come to Tangier, for this new world, what would she think of him now? What could she think now that she was dead? At least she was dead and could no longer see him, or at least he liked to think she could not see him.

Belquassim was sitting next to the front door of the bar along with several other boys of the city. Sitting on his haunches on the ash-covered floor. Just looking at the others it appeared to be all the same. Six or seven young boys leaning against the dark wooden door, most of them under twenty, all dressed in white cotton *djellaba*s. Some of them were dirtier than others, dirt under a small fingernail, black soles of feet, mucus in the corner of an eye. Some had the pained expression of children who have seen too much sex and violence, others were carefree and unconcerned about dark and wanton nights. And they all laughed a lot. Most of the time they ate majoun or smoked hashish, they inhaled it, they ate it. And then they exhaled or spat out their dreams. Occasionally one of the boys would take out his tube of Vaseline and smear the oily colourless lubricant meaningfully over his fingers, grease on his hands. They all had tubes of Vaseline in their pockets, the Vaseline that you could buy cheaply from the Indian chemist up on the Boulevard Pasteur. A half-filled tube meant that too much Vaseline had been wasted in trying to attract a customer, or it meant there was no need to work much more that evening. But they all knew that when the tube was empty, for whatever reason, it meant that you could go home. Belquassim leaned his head against the wall and thought of the man last night. The one who smelled of a lime-flavoured cologne and who had thought he was underage. The man whose hands shook as he undid the buttons of his European trousers. Belquassim had tried to reassure him, had said he was twenty, it was just that he looked younger. He had said that he was fine and that all the boys in Tangier did this. He thought of the hurried way in which the man pulled down his pants in the black alley behind the market store where in the mornings the women would sell peaches and roses. The trousers hung down covering his ankles, how fast he wanted to be. Belquassim didn't need the Vaseline that time, and the man was quick and generous. As he blinked he could taste the milky semen in the back of his throat, it tasted of uncooked fish and black pepper. He could feel it drip down his chin and onto his white shirt. He could smell fear and semen, an enticing combination.

Belquassim looked up at the three people who walked into the bar. They came from the back streets, through the back entrance, through the passage that led not to the beach but to the alley behind the hotel. This could only mean that they knew the streets of the city, they were not just visitors. The back way was hidden from the public, between the fleshy skin of the muddy yellow houses. Not many people really knew the small crooked street that would take a person out of the *souk* and onto the beach. Not many knew of the road that took you to this entrance of the bar. Belquassim had only seen one of them before, the thin man, nervous-looking, with red weals down the insides of both his arms. He wore a hat. He always wore a black hat and a black shirt with long sleeves. Belquassim had seen the wounds when he had wound up the sleeves in the heat of the bar. Otherwise they remained drawn down and buttoned at the wrist. Paul, whose name he did not know until later that night, and the thin man were laughing. Belquassim also laughed, laughed spontaneously, because the sound of Paul's laugh appeared to catch him like a disease. Yellow hair, almost white in the dim light of the bar, covered Paul's head, and as he laughed he leaned into the shoulder of the woman who was with them. He held her with his laughter. She was small and dark, she laughed with the white-haired man, not the same infectious laughter, but the laughter of a child. Her laughter moved up into Belquassim's thighs winding itself into his soft hairless chest. His child's chest. He watched her laugh, then he watched her laugh with the white-haired man. The three of them sat down at the bar, the thin man called out to the bartender and asked for whiskies all round. The barman poured the liquid into the glasses, it swirled gold. Paul looked around him. He looked at the boys in the corner. In a flurry small hands delved into pockets, Vaseline tubes were caressed longingly, but Belquassim kept still. He thought he had heard the voice before, it was reminiscent of something he had experienced somewhere but he could not tell where. He could not hear words, he could just hear the voice. Maybe the voice was in his head. Maybe the stories were his stories. The barman poured out more whiskies. Glasses were raised to open mouths. Suddenly the woman-child got up and came towards the boys. Once again she laughed. "Who can tell me a story?" she asked them in French, "I am bored with the stories my friends tell me, I want something from someone new, something in French, something that I can write for my husband so that he does not get bored with me and my stories." Her eyes moved quickly over all of them, the boys said nothing. Belquassim noticed that a thin line of ants trailed up the wall behind her head. The dividing line. Belquassim looked up from the ants and into her eyes. Her elongated eyes were brown and, as she turned her head and they caught the light, they became a greeny yellow.

"I can tell you stories that have been told to me by others," Belquassim said in English. His voice shook as he tried to sound bold, brazen even. "But because they are old I must speak them in Moghrebi first before I make them into French."

"No-one can tell a story that is his own," she replied. "We all have a common story, it's the same story, an old story, but I want you to tell me anyway. I want you to tell me because you have a new face and therefore you will tell the story differently." Then she leaned down and he smelled the smoky smell of a woman's body, an unfamiliar smell to him now. Her pearl necklace grazed his cheek, one white bead moved across his mouth, he wanted to catch it and hold it between his lips. She took his hand and pulled him over to where the two men were sitting at the bar. Now there were four, the three of them and Belquassim. Her hand was small and moist, it was as if she were afraid.

At first Belquassim felt fear. What did they want from him? Maybe a story meant something else, something that he did not know about. And he knew of the dangers of his work. Only two days before his friend from his village in the Rif had been beaten by someone – he would not say who it was, a pimp, a customer or a Moroccan who hated and despised boy whores. His face had been swollen, his eyes black and filled with damage. But he went back to work anyway. Some customers liked the rough look, it meant the possibility of more.

Then Belquassim thought: But if it really was only a story that they wanted it would be quicker and easier than sex, and not dangerous. All he would have to do was speak. He still sat there. Then Paul was leaning over and whispering into his ear. Through the sounds of voices and the garish music of the European dance halls Belquassim thought he heard Paul say, "Tell me the story, just tell it to me, trust me. I want the story because I am writing music for cello. I want to feel the sound of your voice so that I can write the notes for a cello, those languid cello notes, never too high, but never low. The voice of a boy." And now he felt bold. Yet first he could not think what he would say, what story he would tell – he seemed to have so many.

Then he started to speak of his mother. His mother who had once been beautiful and who would hold him close to her breasts. His nose was in her long dark hair that hung over her shoulders, smelling the sweetness of oil and fragrance. He spoke about how she sat weaving the intricate carpets in the dark coolness of their one-roomed home. The movement of her left hand as she wound the wool over the loom, while her right hand moved back and forth, with emerald, red, yellow, and the black for the border. The way she bit her fingernails, and said her prayers at the tombs of the saints. The colour of her hair, the lines on her lovely ravaged face. Her image was distant but he tried hard to keep it in his mind. He needed her now as he had never needed her before. He needed her smell and the feel of her hair on his cheek.

But soon he realised that what he said was not important. Paul was not interested in the content of his story, just that he spoke, just that. And Paul listened, and put his fingers over the woman's lips when she tried to interrupt, or when she laughed too loudly. And so Belquassim spoke, sometimes about his mother, sometimes about the women in the marketplace and sometimes just about the city.

Much later that night they left the bar together. They went to Paul's house, or Paul and Jane's house, for that was her name, the slim dark woman with the changeable vacant eyes, the slim dark woman who was Paul's wife. And afterwards in the hot air of the open veranda above the house, when the tube of Vaseline was pressed flat, finished, and Belquassim lay leaning into Paul's shoulder on the long bed, Jane brought them small cups of hot coffee. This was not the last time that she would do this, she would do it often. Then she would sit on the floor next to the bed and tell them stories, love stories.

And so Belquassim stayed with Paul and Jane, and sometimes Cherifa, and sometimes the others whom Jane would bring home. He too would make Jane coffee and they would laugh together and count on their fingers the number of people they had fucked in Tangier. And she would tell him about Paul, how they had met, what they ate in America, New York City, but never when they were going back. And when Paul was not at home and there was no other woman with her they would lie together, smoking, waiting for Paul. Belquassim would brush her short dark hair, so that streaks of light appeared in it.

And they only ever went to the bar in the Hotel Mirador together, the three of them.

III

I think of myself as a writer now. "A writer ..." I like the term. It's as good as "nothing". But "nothing" is much too languid, has no intrinsic resonance for me. Why I say this, I suppose, is because my writing is based on nothing – that nothingness that creates existence. It sounds contradictory, nothing creates, but in fact from a kind of nothingness, from my equanimity of just existing, comes an interpretation, or a perception, that can set my writing apart from that of others. It's not clouded by personal feelings or emotions; it just sets existence out, as it is, bleak and beautiful. My experiences have value because I can see the world with clarity, I can see it for what it is. The value that I bring to my work is my lack of feeling, my lack of entanglement and my ability to just pick up and move on. I do not care about anything; that is my value. I never speak about feelings, I do not experience that inner turmoil that most people seem to experience. I do not have feelings. I am able to stand outside the circle, never moving inside. In this way I can capture the feelings of others. I survive by words.

Last night was interesting. Jane, Bill and I went to the Hotel Mirador. I love the bar in the hotel. It has a desperate quality to it. The bar itself is set against the windows, which are long and reach to the floor. Someone who sits there is forced to look out, and what does he see through these windows? The mountain ranges of Spain. It's almost as if we can never get away, any of us. Something else is always there looming large, close, but not close enough to reach out and touch. The mountain range across the sea halts our movement. And the sea in between engulfs. The bar is always full of expatriates and young boys. It really does have the feel of the International Zone, Tangier, owned by no-one, least of all its indigenous people. The bar is a mini replica of Tangier, local boys mixing with foreigners, all of whom have no real existence. The boys because they have left their culture and their homes to sell sex for money, and the foreigners because the very reason we all came to Tangier was to be outside of that world which is supposed to give us meaning. No-one in that bar has any essential identity, we all just exist.

I love Bill and Jane, for I suppose that feeling of familiarity can be called love. They are two people with whom I feel familiar enough to talk. Bill and his bleak sense of humour and cadaverous look. He is a walking corpse, his face has cheekbones that could slice an apple in half. He has just stepped out of a grave. And the way he writes, his words placing on paper experiences that no-one admits exist. The way he put his book together – he threw the pages in the air and then collected them up in a pile, and that was its sequence. Allen then collected the pages and put them into a printable form. Or that is what Bill says, I never trust anything he says. Now people write about the book's unique structure. The way the words fall about in contradictions, the out-of-body experiences that have a tangible physical effect. The desperation to be out of this reality, the desperation to create another. And I love Jane. Who wouldn't? She is filled with life. Her blood is warm. She moves her emotions as one would move furniture. She embraces life. Maybe that's why I married her, so that I could experience life through her, feel her feelings. It's the only way I really know what feelings are all about – her emotions, her fears. It's her desperateness that just pulls me along, her desperate need to fill herself up with life's emotional content. She will live and live and live forever. But love, what is it really? Black solitariness is in my head. And to love ... do I even know what it means?

We were having fun, the three of us. I was talking about the symphony that I am writing for Peggy. It has to be finished by the end of spring, Peggy wants to use it in some play or other on Broadway. New York City, so far away, but not far enough. It encroaches on me even here. I was telling them of the trouble I am having with the cello, and Jane was saying how bored she was with my bleak stories, and Bill, he was just laughing and pretending to be the philosopher. His topic is always the same, or variations on the same theme – the cage of America, and the social murders that happen in the land where he was born. Sometimes it is amusing, at other times it makes me yawn. Then Jane hit on an idea. We could fulfil both our desires at once.

We could get a boy to tell us a story. I could listen to his voice: the Arabs have a melodious quality to their voices, it is a unique, elusive sound that can't really be captured by anything else. Maybe I would be inspired by the sound of that voice to write the music. And she ... she would listen to the story, and maybe the story would inspire her to write. Bill, I don't know what part he thought he would play in the game. Oh, yes, he just said that he wanted to watch, and maybe he would take the boy home and sleep with him afterwards, so Jane had better pick out a pretty boy. Not that it matters much to Bill – what the boy looks like, that is.

Jane walked over to the corner where the boys sat. They all just sit there. Their look is so vacant that you can't imagine that they think. Blank bleak faces, that's maybe why I like them, their outer self reflects my inner self. Anyway she picked out one of them and brought him to the bar. A pretty boy. His eyes were elongated, almost oriental, set against his dark mouth. I think he painted his eyes to get his expression. He was tall and thin. And he spoke, and, what did he speak of? I never heard a word of his story, something about his mother I think, but it was not the story I was interested in, but his voice, the sound as it emerged from his slow wide mouth. The sound inspired me to listen. It lifted him upwards, the accent was half Moroccan, half International Zone, half nothing, It rose and fell in like an angel riding a wave, and amid the din and racket of the bar I heard a music that I have seldom encountered in a voice. Peggy will be pleased that I found him. He made the sounds of the cello for her.

I took him home with me. I just wanted to hear more of him. His voice seemed to glide up and around me, I also wanted to hear him gasp in pain and pleasure. Why, because that is another sound. I don't much care for sex, which is why I do not often get involved with it. Taking pleasure from the body is absurd – it ties one to thinking that life is to be enjoyed – but anyway I wanted to hear the sounds. Much later on, after Jane had made us some of that strong Arabic coffee that she likes so much, we went to sleep. Or at least Belquassim went to sleep, that is his name, Belquassim. It's a beautiful name. I must write it down so that I remember it. At first I did not want him to sleep, I wanted to go on touching his skin so that I could hear the sounds that he would make. But he is young, and he, I suppose, was tired, and so

Belquassim slept. I say the name again. And even his breathing in the darkened room seemed like music to me. I always know what time it is in the night when I cannot sleep for the sounds are different at different times. First it is the cicadas that supposedly only rub their legs together when they want to have sex, but they seem to do it every night. They need to be tied to life, I suppose, as their lives are so short that they need to obtain immortality by breeding a lot. Although I often wonder if they just have sex every night because they enjoy the sound. And then it's the rustle of the lizard on the ceiling. In the dark, at about three o'clock in the morning he, the lizard that is, starts his mad dance on the ceiling, walking upside down above my head. I wonder how he manages to stay on the ceiling. There is a scientific reason for it, but who can accept a scientific reason, so dull really, so rooted in logic? When I turn the light on he disappears. I have never seen this ghost of a lizard, I have only heard him. He is always there. Then at first light I hear the sounds of the street, and the muezzin calling, waking, "Allahu Akbar. As-salatu jayrun min an nawn. La ilaha illa illah." I lay and listened to Belquassim breathing and wrote down the music for the cello in my head. I think it will be magnificent. I felt the notes in that soft skin beside me breathing.

ﯼﯾ

I vacillate between extravagant happiness and numb despair. There is some equilibrium that operates when the other two feelings are not present, but I can count these moments of equilibrium on my fingers, whereas the other two are innumerable. At the moment it is the extravagant happiness part that I feel.

I love this city – even the name, Tangier, has a ring to it. And the International Zone. I cannot rationalise its existence politically. No-one who thinks, I believe, can ever rationalise colonialism in any form. It is only the faceless patriot who believes in the right of conquest and subjugation. Or is it (sometimes I am not certain) colonising others? Perhaps we all do it without recognising what it is. Am I colonising Cherifa, or is she colonising me? But I love the city for that lack of morality that it has. No-one, at least no-one of the expatriates, imposes a judgement upon anything or anyone. Everyone is somehow outside of social morality. I can move from the streets of the souks where women sit day after day working, selling, bartering, to the cafés where the men are permanently stoned on hash or majourn, to the places where the expatriates get drunk. And everyone just carries on living; it is as if they know that judgement here is of no force and effect and so it just passes them by. I am not obsessed with making judgements, or having them imposed upon me, like Bill is for instance. But no, that is a lie. I am obsessed with being judged, that is where the bleak despair comes from, that's why I like the city, it is free of what I most hate. Except of course when the despair comes again, then I can hate anywhere, then I just hate where I am.

I love Paul. I will love him forever. But he says he has never loved anyone. How can I love someone who does not love me back? He always says "You are not I. So you love and I will not." He has colonised me, or have I allowed this colonisation, as some say of the Moroccans? They allowed it to happen, as they knew that they would gain much from the French. They wanted it. They were lesser than their masters were. Am I lesser than Paul? Is he my master? Paul has taken my heart, something like what a photograph does for the Arabs – when you take a photograph you take a part of a person's soul. He stands outside of me and takes a photograph, and therefore has my soul. It is his, no matter how hard I try I cannot give it to anyone else. Futile, maybe. How can you give your soul to someone who is so impassive, who never shows a feeling no matter what? But I gave it to him, and even if he remains forever an enigma, love is not rational. I rationalise to myself daily, telling myself that he loves me, but at the end its does not matter for the feelings are as irrational as the moment. When we touch each other, it is passion mixed with my emotions and his lack of emotion that I love most of all. It is the way he touches me, touches my skin. Skin on skin. And we don't have sex any more.

It is 1949, he has just finished his first book. Is Paul brilliant? I can never write like he does. He tries to encourage me to write. I have written one book, which I think is probably the best book that has ever been written, but that was then, and that was the end of it. What an achievement, one brilliant book! Well they are lucky that I wrote it after all. Now in a sense he has taken over my role. He is the writer now. And after all what are words anyway. To me, they mean nothing *as long as I have my feelings, both the good and the bad ones. I do not need to describe them. I just want to feel.*

IV

Paul leaned forward. His white hair fell over his face as he turned the pages of the manuscript that he was reading from. Now and then he would lift his hand and brush it away, so that he could still see the words written on the pages. Occasionally he would lean down and pick up the hash pipe that lay on the floor next to the bed and breathe in the smoke, drawing it far into his lungs and then releasing it slowly. He had been reading to Belquassim for a long time. It seemed as if he had been reading the whole night, whereas in fact it had only been for less than an hour. The hash slowed Paul's voice down, it slowed down time. On and on it went until the lines that he read seemed to blur in Belquassim's head. It was a story about three travellers to Algeria, two men and one woman. A desert story. The woman in the story seemed to be Jane. Paul had told him that he used many women as his model for Kit, for that was the name of the woman in the story, but somewhere Belquassim knew that she was Jane. It was about travel through the desert, moving from one arid red town to another. The long nights on trains, buses filled with people, the mint tea in different market places and the flies that alighted on their faces as they slept, biting hardest where the skin was broken. He knew that Port, Kit's husband, would die of typhoid. He would die in an empty French barrack outside a small town. And the wind blew incessantly in that town, it blew through the empty room in which he lay. He would die alone without his wife, she who could not cope with the transience of life. She who had left him alone so as not to have to think about him. Belquassim spent a long time telling Paul of the time that his sister was ill, the long night fevers, the delirium and the slow development of her hatred as death came closer. This was how Port would die. Kit, after the death of her husband, then left more than just his body, she left her senses behind. She left her America and became part of a caravan that was moving its silver across the desert. She left behind her civilisation, her body-wrapped right-mindedness, to appropriate another civilisation, one that inflicted a suffering that she could never previously have known, but one that allowed her to revel with an almost sensuous pleasure in her own suffering and to understand that it is only death that can claim ownership. It was the end of the road. This was how Paul described it to him as they lay there on the bed in Erfoud. But more important to Belquassim was that Kit's Bedouin lover had the same name as he did, this is what he remembered most of all. He could repeat Paul's words, but what he remembered most of all was the name, his name. He felt alive in the pages of the story. It was a story of trust and betrayal. It was a love story. And he was the lover.

They were lying in bed in a small hotel in a town at the edge of the Sahara, Erfoud. It was bitterly cold outside as it was December, in fact nearly January, it was 31 December, and winter. The hotel, one of the two in the town, was bleak, its walls stained with many nights of smoke and conversation. The car that they had used to drive down in was parked at the back of the building. It had been difficult to move the car into the space, as it was crowded with people and camels, traders from the desert. Small fires loomed out of the dark and the fetid insecure breath of the camels engulfed them as they parked the car and walked into the hotel. The hotel had a small communal area at its entrance. You had to walk up several stairs from the yard to get inside. At the entrance hung a long Bedouin blanket to keep out the wind and the cold, but it blew in anyway and it was very cold. In the entrance several people sat drinking and smoking, waiting for midnight. Lots of people, the faces stared at them as they entered, white and brown masks, only the eyes following them as they crossed the floor. Paul wanted to go to their room before coming out for supper. Belquassim knew that he wanted to feel his slim skin, he wanted to be touched by Belquassim's hands, he wanted to guide himself into Belquassim so that he could hear him gasp. Belquassim followed Paul, he could do nothing else. They went to the bedroom, he felt Paul's hair on his neck. He heard his own spontaneous cry. And he heard the match light up and saw the flame balanced on the edge of the pipe. Paul did not speak nor did he moan with pleasure. Afterwards Paul leaned across him and with his forefinger traced his own name with Belquassim's semen across the flat brown stomach. Belquassim could feel the letters "P-A-U-L," The semen smelled of pimentos and when he put his fingers into it to taste it, it tasted salty.

Belquassim leaned his head against Paul's shoulder as he read. Almost as if by reflex, Paul raised his hand from the pages and pushed aside the collar of his camel wool jacket so that the flesh of his neck and shoulder was exposed. His flesh was soft and white, it felt like his voice, soft and caressing. The reflex movement signified a sense of comfort to Belquassim, there was no need to ask any questions, he was a part of Paul's life, like the life that had by now grown dry on his stomach. They lay like this for a long time, Paul reading, Belquassim leaning his head against Paul's shoulder.

They had come to Erfoud to see the sun rise over the winter desert. Paul wanted to feel the cold wind eat into his face and then feel the sun melt the cold away as it moved into his shoulders and face. He wanted to describe this in his book. He needed this experience. Belquassim had negotiated with a young guide, Yacoubi, in the *souk* before they arrived at the hotel to take them many miles into the desert. They were to rise early the next day so that they could see the sun rise. New Year, new day, new sun, new story, thought Belquassim as he lay there, becoming sleepy, almost like a dream, he heard a bell ring. Paul looked down at him, closed the pages of the manuscript slowly, so slow. He leaned across and kissed Belquassim. Quietly on the mouth. Then he ran his hand down across Belquassim's shoulder and over his chest, that thin brown hairless chest, before getting up. "Sometimes you make me want emotions so I can love you," Belquassim thought he heard Paul murmur, but he could not be sure. And then all he could hear was the splashing of the water in the basin and Paul's exclamation as he felt its icy tentacles reach out across his face. Belquassim believed in love, his love for Paul. And he knew that Paul loved the experiences that they shared, for they reacted similarly to them. But he also knew that, long ago, Paul had built a cage, a cage to save himself from love. And there was no key to this cage. And he tried and tried and tried, but nothing, no key that he ever found could move the cage door.

They walked out of the room together down the passage and into the hotel's communal entrance. The proprietor was Spanish. He was busy serving the New Year meal to the other guests. He beckoned them forward and showed them where to sit. They sat in the middle on low-set cushions next to three women who looked American. It was noisy in the entrance. Paul smiled at the women and greeted them in French. Most people spoke French in these parts, the Europeans and the Arabs alike. Two of the women just stared at him while the other greeted him. Her accent was like Paul's, American. Did they already know each other? All three of the women looked as if they had been travelling a long while. Their white blouses tucked into cotton skirts were streaked with the dust of the tourist, or was it the dust of the missionary? It was in the creases and lines on their faces. Their eyes were dusted over with fatigue. One wore a blue Bedouin shawl over her head, to keep the wind out. The indigo from the cloth stained her cheeks a dark blue. They are probably older than they look, thought Belquassim, but he didn't care one way or the other, he was not really interested in them. He looked only at Paul. And Paul looked at the women. His eyes moving lackadaisically over their bodies, appraising, examining, making up words. Belquassim knew this habit of Paul's, he was describing them to himself, putting them down in a picture, taking away their humanity and their tiredness and the way in which they thought they were all right.

The food was served in small pottery bowls. A steaming hot tagine. Belquassim dipped the thick bread into the juice of the stew, the lamb was fatty and the juice ran down his chin. He wiped it off with the back of his hand and licked his fingers. The oily juice tasted salty and smelled of pimentos. The Spanish proprietor seemed to be continually moving – this one, that one, always someone wanting something else – moving to nowhere. The smell of the hashish pipe contributed to the somnambulant feel of the meal. Smoke drifted upwards and sideways. It curled yellow around the blanket that covered the door and drifted out to the men and the camels in the parking ground. In the corner of the room a young boy started to beat a drum. Ta ta ta ta, ta ta ta ta ta ta ta ... Belquassim laughed in time to the beat and ate more of the stew. The couscous looked like little round beads glistening in the oiliness of the meat. Paul and the three women were now talking. They seemed to barely hear the boy on the drum. It was as if Paul wanted to forget the last hour that he had spent with Belquassim, maybe the women reminded him of Jane, maybe he needed a woman's affirmation. Belquassim could look at them no longer so he looked at the young drummer. He seemed to be part girl, part boy. It was the way he focused on the faces of the nameless people in the room, the simple flirtatiousness of the boy with the wisdom of a young girl. Belquassim wondered what the boy did for a living. Playing a drum could not bring in much in a hotel so far away from the world. Maybe he did what Belquassim did, or what he used to do before he met Paul, but in this town, with whom? The drum beat on, the sound moved faster, whirling round and round. The boy smiled at him, a knowing smile, and Belquassim laughed again. The drum beat on. The boy's sour breath reached Belquassim as he stopped drumming for a moment to adjust the long black *burnous* that encircled his head. And then it started again, Ta ta ta ta, ta ta ta ta ta ta ta ... And so it beat on into the wind and into the night.

Soon the meal was finished, but the smoke was not. Paul offered the women a pipe but they nervously refused. Paul laughed at them and said to the woman with the turban over her head, "It's control isn't it? You don't want to lose control. Why not? Tell me what framework you need to cling to. Here you can control nothing, and why should you want to? Tell me what it means to you to be so far away from all that you know. Tell me what it means to you to be always trying to convince others that you are right." She did not reply. Belquassim thought she looked afraid, as if her clothes were torn from her. She looked as if she wanted something, but she was unable to describe it. Suddenly the boy beating the drum stopped playing and came over to them. He looked at the woman with the turban over her head and the indigo face, but he asked all of them – Belquassim could hear his hollow words, his fractured French – "Do you want something special?" As he spoke he glanced at Paul, but then moved his gaze back to the woman's face. Belquassim did not know whether he was also directing his question at Paul. He knew it was not directed at him.

"What is it that you do in this small town?" Paul asked the drummer. He asked the question not because he was interested, Belquassim knew this by the way that Paul was looking at him, but because it might be a story that he could use later. Paul could change and adapt the story to what he wanted to write.

The drummer looked at Paul, as if he knew that what he said would make no difference to this cold face. "When I play the drum I earn money. When I direct people to this hotel, like I directed these women –" and he pointed at the women as he spoke – "I earn commission from the hotel owner. And I also arrange camel trips in the desert so that I can earn commission."

"So what do you do now when there are only a few tourists around?" Paul asked him.

"I do nothing," the boy replied. "I earn nothing when no-one wants business. But sometimes –" and he laughed showing his yellow teeth to the room "– I arrange the kif. When someone needs kif I can get it for him." And he laughed again. But the conversation was dead. Belquassim could see that the story was of no interest to Paul. And the boy was not really interested in Paul or the commission he might get from him.

In Moghrebi Belquassim joked with the drummer, some-thing about the drumbeats making him want the women, and that they were richer than Paul was, for the moment at least. And he could get commission, more than commission from one of them. The drummer laughed and winked, he was interested in the one with the indigo face. The one who could not describe her fear. He could sense her fear, it blew off her like a strange smell. He also knew how to persuade and he knew a good buy when he saw one, one with whom he would succeed. Soon they were laughing and talking, half Moghrebi half French. At first the woman was hesitant. Then she opened her mouth tentatively. Then she opened it wider and the French words spilled out from it. It was as if the boy was filling a glass. Little by little the glass became full until the words like the liquid spilled over the edge. Now the drummer's hand was on her knee, moving in slow circles, sometimes under the material of her skirt, sometimes just on top of it. And she did nothing. Her eyes betrayed her need and her voice her fear. Who would be the winner in this conflict of need and fear? Belquassim watched Paul as he watched the terrible theatre play itself. Maybe this would be a story?

Belquassim smiled at Paul. Above the sound of the voices Paul said, "In my book I describe two terrible tourists, a stupid fat American mother and her stupid fat American son, incestuous, they fuck each other, but I can't seem to find the images. Do you think I can use these women in my description? They have the American accent, that uncouth sound of a bigot? They have no sensuality, only rules and counter rules if the first ones don't work. It is remarkable how Americans are able to rationalise their existence. And the drummer," he went on, "he has the right look for my caravan driver. He is dark and dressed in black, a little young. Although he does have that turban wrapped around his head … he looks a bit, a bit like the young Byron. Do you think he also has a limp? His deformity, an emotional cripple."

Belquassim said quietly, "But I thought your caravan driver looked like me, he has my name."

"He has your name only because your name is beautiful." Paul replied. "My young camel driver, like you? How can he be like you?"

Much later they left. The drummer too had left the cold dining entrance and the women had gone to their rooms. Need or fear, who was the winner? Belquassim wondered as he and Paul walked down the cold dark passageway. The new year had come, it was now January. It was still cold. Paul leaned close into him while he slept. Belquassim knew that he loved Paul. And as love was not a word that he took for granted, it made him afraid. The sound of the drumbeat ... with the wind, slipping slowly through the window and over the dun-coloured camel hair blanket that lay on top of them ... The drumbeat crept into his heart ... but then, with sleep, it stopped as insignificantly as it had started ... A young boy with saturnine breath wearing a black turban sat in the corner and watched.

In the morning when the car horn sounded Paul and Belquassim were still asleep. It was dark. The basin had frozen over in the night. Quickly they roused each other. Paul lit the oil lamp that was on the table next to the bed. He leaned out of the window and beckoned the guide to be quiet, they would be down soon. Quickly they dressed. The lamplight cast shadows over Paul's face as he bent down to pull on his boots. Then he threw some water over himself. Belquassim thought he saw a smile play across Paul's face. A life flitted across Paul's chin and then trickled down his neck with the broken shards of the icy water. They walked lightly down the stairs so as not to wake anyone and then left through the blanket on the door.

The old car snorted in the cold. The guide, Yacoubi, smoked a cheroot. Paul asked him for one. "I need it to keep me awake, it makes my heart beat faster, so I think that I am getting more oxygen into my brain," he said. Yacoubi drove them to the outskirts of the town where they were to meet his brother. His brother was to provide them with the camels for the journey into the desert. Ten minutes later they reached a compound outside the town. Yacoubi's brother and a woman were waiting for them. He looked older than he was, the sand had etched its story into his cheeks. The woman's face was covered. She wore a turban wound around her head and a *haik* covered her face. Across her eyes was a band of gold mesh. She was invisible. The money changed hands, Yacoubi wound a *burnous* over Paul's head, the Bedouin way, and then Paul and Belquassim climbed onto the seated camel. Belquassim sat in front, Paul behind him. The woman and Yacoubi's brother rode the other camel, her hands resting lightly on his hips, her covered face pressed against his shoulder. Yacoubi walked silently next to them.

The camels moved slowly. Yacoubi walked next to the animals. Occasionally he would lightly hit them with a thin whip-like cane to keep them moving in the right direction. He seemed not to tire even though he never rode, just walked, silently and resolutely forward. Belquassim leaned into his camel's neck, it was like being on a boat. The camel swayed in the darkness, moving him onwards through the tide. He could have fallen asleep again except he knew that if he did this he might fall. He felt Paul's arms tighten around his waist, he saw the sky over his head, which could not shelter him from the cold, and pushed himself backwards, closer into Paul's embrace. And so they moved onwards. For a long time he did not change his position, he just felt Paul's arms tighten around him. Swaying as if on a boat.

They moved onwards through the sand. Slowly the dark was eaten away by the sun. Little by little, as he looked around him he saw small pieces of yellow following the camel's strides. They seemed to get longer the more he looked. Little bits of yellow eating into the sand and pushing the darkness back. The only sound was the sound of the camel, and occasionally Yacoubi would spit, his spittle leaving a small paw-print in the enveloping desert.

"Look," said Paul. Belquassim pushed his head up and out of the folds of his *djellaba*. The sun was moving upwards, edging over the dune ahead of them. It was more than just a ray now, now it seemed to fill the whole of the desert, it covered the sand so that its long cast shadows appeared like a cloth that was wound around a woman's body. The sun seemed to speak, or maybe it was actually singing. He thought he could see the voices of the dead in the shadows that grew wider and wider as the sun rose. The voices of the dead poets whose poetry Paul had read to him, the voice of his sister. But he could hear no words, he could just feel them in the sun's rays. The cold filled his lungs as he took in a breathless breath, and the sun warmed him. He could feel one of Paul's cold hands across his stomach; it seemed to get warmer as the sun rose higher.

They were to travel for three days, and then they were to return to Erfoud. Far into the desert, Paul wanted to hear its silence, Belquassim wanted to hear Paul describe its silence.

As the dawn broke over the horizon Belquassim thought he heard Paul gasp. He felt him lean over the side of the camel, he was trying to reach for something in the bags that hung down the side of the long body but he could not get to it. Paul called to Yacoubi to stop. Belquassim heard Yacoubi exchange a brief sentence with his brother, before turning to Paul to say that they could not. They had to move forward before the day began, as even though it was winter the sun would not be friendly for much longer. They had to move forward quickly so that they could get to a small oasis where they would spend the rest of the day in the shade before they once again leaned into the wind of the night.

After what seemed a long time Belquassim saw that they were following a line of small shrubs. The plants rolled in the sand as the legs of the camels brushed against them. It was as if they were following a river, but the river lay deep under the sand. A small pool of shadow suddenly appeared against the horizon. The shadow seemed to get closer as the camel swayed. And then they were at the oasis. A few brown houses were set around the well. But the area was small. A child-woman dressed in black walked with a donkey around the water; a camel-skin bucket tied to the end of the rope. The donkey moved around and around the water pulling it upwards. Once the bucket came to the lip of the water the woman would empty it into a larger container. And then the donkey would begin its journey again. It had walked this circle for centuries. Yacoubi set up the small tent and blanket in a corner, in the grey shadow of one of the small structures. But the shade was little, not enough for the five of them to sit in. The water of the oasis looked brown. Yacoubi coaxed to its knees the camel that his brother and the invisible woman rode. Then he came over and coaxed to its knees the camel that Belquassim and Paul rode. Paul held onto Belquassim as the camel slid downwards, Belquassim leaned back into Paul to steady him. Yacoubi placed a blanket on the small stretch of sand. He beckoned to them and told them to lie down, it was to be a long day. The woman lit a fire for tea. Soon Belquassim could smell the strong mint and sugar. She handed around some broken glasses and filled them with the pungent sweet liquid. And they drank. The blanket was coarse and pricked Belquassim's skin through his shirt. He lay down nonetheless knowing that he should rest. Paul lay down next to him and pushed his face into Belquassim's waist. "It is the smell," he said to Belquassim, "I want to smell myself in you through the smell of the blanket." Belquassim closed his eyes.

When they had rested for what seemed hours Paul got up. He started to move outside and beyond the small oasis area. "Hai ...!" called Yacoubi, "Don't move too far, you will get lost." Paul glanced at him and walked from the circle of shade. Belquassim watched him as he moved outwards but did not follow him. He was afraid, afraid of the engulfing desert sand. Despite his love he could not overcome the fear of this heat and the lost space. Sometime later Paul returned to the group. "I needed to hear the silence," was all he said. Belquassim looked into Paul's blue eyes and he knew that this was a memory he could not forget. For a moment he was able to forget about loneliness. He was able to forget about being alone in the desert.

Later as twilight came down across the sand dunes Yacoubi and his brother started to pack up. The woman handed round some hard dry meat. Belquassim ate. And then they got up onto the camels and were once again rolling with the hot dry wind. A bright moon started to rise, replacing the sun. Its rays were as bright, but cold. Belquassim watched it rise, the soft yellow glow mesmerised him as the sun could not do. He watched it carve a path across the star-littered sky, making its mark in the hemisphere. Now and again a bird or a bat would fly across the light, a piece of blackness against the light, and then it would fly onwards. And the moon remained, travelling through the sky.

The same pattern was repeated for three days. The journey

on the camels in the night, sleeping, reading, and for Paul, writing, during the day. Paul seemed content to just watch the sand and the sky, and then, when it was time to sleep, he would put his hands under Belquassim's loose fitting shirt or into his Bedouin pants and they would lie there. Silent. During the nights as they were travelling Paul would tell him about what he was writing. The harshness of the desert seemed to bring out different words, words that in the city he could not articulate. A mixture of dust and heat and savageness, but tinged with a strange softness that Belquassim did not recognise. Words about the never-ending sky that embraced them with blue during the day and with black during the night. The erotic, interminable, relentless sky. Sometimes Paul's words were realised in their silent passion, sometimes Paul would just speak them out to him. And the sheltering sky remained overhead. And behind the sky was blackness.

V

At the compound just outside Erfoud where we were to meet the camel driver a strange thing happened. I saw a man standing next to his old beat-up car. Beat up, the beat movement, I wonder if that's where Allen got the term from, beat up, not new, not really acceptable, yet moving onwards nonetheless. The Beat Generation, they are already calling it that. But I digress, the man next to the car was young, he must have been in his early thirties, he was a taxi driver. Another man, he looked very old, but I could hardly see him as he was covered from head to toe with a burnous. *But it looked as if the old man was trying to negotiate a ride with the taxi driver to somewhere. The old man seemed to speak endlessly, I could hear a little of what he was saying, as I was close enough to the car. The young man was getting impatient, I could tell by his expression. The old man did not have enough money for the ride. Suddenly the taxi driver slammed the car door closed, the old man had his hand in the doorframe. His hand was caught in the door. The old man opened the door with his other hand, his finger was almost severed to the bone. I could see the blood fall onto the dry sand, and there it lay, red on yellow. Then the old man murmured* "Praise be to Allah" *in Mogrhebi, and walked away. There were no recriminations, nothing.*

Can I have no recriminations when someone harms me? I am uncertain of the extent of my emptiness. And then there was the young boy who played the drum. He had a warped old face, as if time had just passed through him, or maybe passed next door to him. He picked up the American woman's fear. He saw it and moulded it in his hands as if he were making a bowl of clay. Her fear was placed in the mould so that, once moulded, he could take it out and do with it what he wished.

But it is not the people I come here for. I come for the desert. I love the silence out here. It is teaching me something about solitude, about reintegration. I can fight this reintegration of silence if I want to. Sometimes it is difficult not to try to keep hold of the man that I know, the American in me, but I think I have let it take its course. I do not remain who I am. It's not loneliness that I feel – feeling lonely presupposes that one has a memory of not being alone and I have no such memories. Whatever memory I may have had seems to disappear. I hear nothing but my own breathing, and I feel nothing but the blood moving through my veins and up into my brain allowing me to think. After this feeling I can only feel me. Just me, the inside of me. The inside of silence. The inside of nothing.

ৼ

The man with the yellow hair is strange. He hardly speaks, not like a Nazarene at all. They all talk all the time, telling you what to do, thinking that you are unable to do the simplest things and always that their way is better. Sometimes the yellow-haired man just walks off into the desert alone, he leaves his boy behind. I have to warn him not to go far for otherwise he will get lost in the sand. I like the man with the yellow hair, he is not like a Nazarene at all. Sometimes I think that even though he is stupid – what man walks into the desert alone? – I trust him. His hair is the colour of the sand. He will remain here for a long time.

ৼ

Paul and Belquassim have left Tangier and gone to see the sun setting in the Sahara, or maybe it is the sun rising in the Sahara, I am not sure what Paul said. In a way I wanted to go too, I wanted to spend time with Paul. But at the same time I did not want to go with them. It would ruin my time with Paul if he were engaged in something that I detested. I detest him when all he wants to think about is his writing. And I detest the dirt and squalor of these small desert towns. Sometimes I think that the liberty that is afforded to me by being in Tangier is eroded by the social injustices that I see perpetrated everywhere else in the country. Not of course that the city is free from social injustice, but that elsewhere is it just so much more apparent. For instance I see women covered from top to toe in black, only the slits of their eyes showing, and even then sometimes not at all. And they are working, working in the oasis to keep the olive groves from being decimated by the sun. I can feel the sweat that covers them, it glows through the blackness of their gowns and makes strange patterns in the dark material. And I wander freely down a dirt road, free from that restrictive clothing, but also free to think and explore my thinking. I have the experience of liberty, the liberty to indulge in my own freedom. And I can grow. Or can I? Does this freedom give me anything better than what the Moroccan women have? Belquassim talks of the freedom of the haik. Maybe one is freer to explore oneself if no-one knows you except those that are closest to you. But the ones that can grow in this freedom are those who are not plagued by poverty and the need just to survive. I judge them all. Maybe I judge because I am defensive. Maybe I judge because I really do have something more worthwhile. Maybe there is some objective reality that is a yardstick. But I cannot even identify what the yardstick is. And whose yardstick is it. I don't know any more.

All I know is that I am alone in Tangier. I miss Paul. I miss the rules that he lives by, I miss his ability to remain free of judgement, by which he frees me. And I miss his skin. Am I jealous of Belquassim? Not really. He is feeling that skin now, but – and it is so cruel to think it – but I am the one that will feel that skin forever, not Belquassim. He will move on, Paul will move on, and I will move on with him. I wonder to where. I need a snapshot of now so that I can see where we all travel to. I want Cherifa to hold me tonight. I know that she will not do so, she never holds a person she just fucks them. But even though I know that what I feel for her is lust and passion, I want to be fucked by her. But I still want her to hold me. The illusion of skin and closeness, and I need all the illusions that I am able to find. We all do I think. Illusion keeps romance alive.

VI

There were four of them at the table in the bar, Belquassim, Paul, Jane and Bill. Belquassim felt that he and Bill had a bond, Bill was there when he met Paul. Bill was inextricably bound to Paul and therefore he was bound to Belquassim. And Bill distracted Jane. He made her laugh. But Jane was ill again. "It's sort of light-headedness mixed in with nausea," she said, "and sometimes I feel like vomiting up everything, it's churning inside me." But her body and its nausea did not seem to deter her from drinking more whisky. It was the only available whisky in Tangier and it had a sour taste that Belquassim did not enjoy. He was drinking Coke, it had no alcohol in it so he felt that at least he was not mocking his dead sister whose faith had been so important. She may not have liked the company I keep, but at least I am not drinking alcohol, he thought and smiled as Paul's phrase came into his head: "You and your ubiquitous Coke". He took another sip, it was sweet on his tongue and melted like a sugar cube in the back of his throat.

Bill was speaking endlessly about the new book he was writing. He described the detail of his inability to write until he got to Tangier. "Lately," he said, "I am writing as if there is no single day left in my life to write." Would there be a single day left in his life? Belquassim wondered. Bill was so thin and he had running welts down both his arms where he would inject himself with his daily ration of eukodol. He was describing what he had written about that afternoon. "My foot, the sight of my foot as it melted away while I lay on my bed. My toes grew bigger and bigger. I am a schizophrenic junkie." He laughed at his words. "And, well, maybe it will be a great book one day: genius bred out of junk." It seemed to

Belquassim to be an endless discussion that had no meaning. Maybe for the others it meant something, but he could never understand the European fixation with drugs and destruction. He liked to smoke hashish himself, but this was a prelude for sex. It relaxed him, he felt weightless and transparent, and he could not see any other purpose for it. But drugs seemed to have a purpose for Bill. "They are like the fucking thought-police, the bastards," Bill said. "All governments are built on lies … What is the war against drugs except a war against dissent, a war against truth? And truth is very dangerous. Truth is the most dangerous man in America … Who was it that said that again? And I – you think that I flatter myself – but I am making a hole in the big ugly American lie … we, all of us here" – and he opened his arms as if to embrace those that sat around the table – "are making such a big fucking hole because we are dangerous. We are exposing their chains."

"I don't know," said Jane, "I am not sure any more. Maybe it's just that your drugs, your heroin or whatever it is you take, and my whisky …" she held up her glass and beckoned the barman. The glass was empty, it needed to be refilled. "… and my whisky … It makes us all reach into ourselves. It makes us cry, real big tears, genuine tears, not worthless ones, tears that we can cry because we have died already. They make us die and then these substances kill us again. But I know what you mean – because if we don't die, then we will be just the same as all of them. Become the lie. I drink to forget the truth, not to find it."

I know that it is not just for the pleasure, thought Belquassim, but I can't understand it, I can't understand it because I have died enough, I have seen enough death to know how to cry. He turned to Paul, he wondered what he thought, but Paul was far away – his truth or his lies were not there at the bar, or in the whisky that he slowly sipped from the round glass with its chipped edges.

Belquassim loved Jane. In a way he knew he had to because if he did not his love for Paul could no longer exist, it could never be sustained. Paul described his relationship with Jane to

Belquassim. "It is a relationship that few will ever understand," he had told him once, "I think that is a great relationship because it is based on our common understanding, or maybe misunderstanding, of the world. We have an implicit trust which, despite distance and sexual infidelity, will always be there. For Jane I am her harbour, for me, Jane is my harbour. Everyone else is just one of the small ports that we call in to along the way. We always come back to our common city. It may be a city that will destroy us in the end, but we will come back anyway. We will come back always, because – I can't call it love for that is just a word … We come back to each other because, maybe, we fill each other's emptiness. But it is a relationship that is difficult to sustain. It cannot last."

Was he a small port to be called in on along the way? Belquassim wondered. Or were they all just ships trapped in the same harbour? He tried not to resent Jane and her constant presence, but sometimes he just did. Then he would compose poetry for her. Moghrebi poems in which he described her strength, her ability to sing and show Paul his way through his writing, and most of all about her love for Paul. The words that he used in his poetry, he knew now, were vague and foolish and over-dramatic. But these poems had a purity which he seemed unable to capture in anything else he wrote. At times he felt he was an outsider looking in to this perfect love affair, which he knew was not perfect for the world, which he knew could never be perfect. At other times when they were all sitting together around the table he thought that he might just have a part to play in it, a small cameo, at least a second on the stage. Sometimes, after creating these poems, sometimes just a few lines, he would give them to her, she could not read Moghrebi, although she could speak it, but he liked her to know that he had written them for her.

Jane was getting drunker. "She drinks too much," Paul said, seemingly to himself.

Jane took hold of one of Bill's thin hands. "Forget about your feet and your drugs for a minute," she said, "and stop worrying about your writing – think of me when you start to worry. I can't seem to do anything these days, let alone write … And look …" She pointed across the bar. Silhouetted in the doorway out to the road that ran along the beach stood a girl. She looked probably only about fourteen. Belquassim did not know her, but she had the look of someone who was new to the bar in the Hotel Mirador. She looked as if she had been sent to look for someone, she did not belong in this room. She has probably been sent by her mother, thought Belquassim, she has probably been sent to make some money.

Jane smiled at Bill and Belquassim and asked mockingly, "Altogether more interesting than feet, don't you think? Do you think money can buy me love, just for a night at least? And if it can," she continued, "do you have any to lend me? Promise I'll repay you some day."

"Oh, love," Bill was by now in a sentimental mood, or maybe it was sarcastic, "the only real painkiller, the most natural painkiller that there is, that's what love is, better than any morphine that I have ever known."

Paul looked up at Bill as he said this, his eyes narrowing as he stared at the thin death-like face. "You shot your wife in a game. Did you love her enough to kill her?" He continued to no-one in particular, "It's the drugs that are talking. You inject love into those popped out veins of yours so that you can believe in it. Your love drug." Belquassim looked at Paul. There was no judgement in his expression, either in his voice or on his face. He was just observing what he saw.

Bill was stoned and Jane was drunk. She had that slightly hysterical laugh that Belquassim knew so well. The laugh that told him that every moment she had was precious. Soon she would either fall against Paul's chest and sleep, or she would want to find something or someone to play with. Belquassim wished Jane would not drink so much, he saw how it tired Paul to keep watching her. Watching her to keep her safe. Belquassim wanted Paul's attention, he wanted to hear more about his stories, and the poets and the writers – they filled his fantasies now. He did not want to watch Paul watching, to be watching Paul's vigilance – watching him step outside the circle to watch.

By now the conversation at the table had turned to the topic of happiness. It had started with a question. Belquassim had said to Jane, "Are you happy?"

She had looked at him with that strange haunted look that she sometimes wore and said, "No, of course I am not happy. Happiness is such a mediocre state of being. I have periods of extravagant happiness when I want the feeling to go on and on and on. And then I go through periods of excruciating, debilitating depression when the sides of the world seem to sink in on me. My heart beats, I panic and I cannot breathe. But while I am not happy, and do not want to be happy, I am interesting. I am interested in me. And that, my darling, is what I think, for what it's worth," and she laughed. "Today I am extravagantly happy, tomorrow, who knows?" She looked up at Belquassim and smiled. "But you, I want you to be happy," she said, "because that is a nice thing to wish for someone."

And the girl still hovered like a bird in the doorway. Jane called her over to the table. "Let's try to make her happy. Maybe she will make me happy just for one night," she said to no-one in particular. The girl came forward. She had a naive animal look, her eyes did not look into the eyes of others, they moved constantly in the light. She spoke quickly to Belquassim in Moghrebi. She had been sent to the bar, but not by her mother. She had been sent by Cherifa to find Jane. Cherifa was not happy and she wanted Jane at home, she hated the bars. Belquassim relayed this message to Jane. Jane got up, she swayed heavily into Bill. "So much for feet," she whispered to him, "I have something better at home. I have that natural painkiller you speak so eloquently about."

Bill looked up with glazed eyes. He watched her move. She could barely walk. "Yes," Bill muttered, "shoot it in the mainline, hits like a speedball, can't miss."

Jane leaned against the young girl's body, she was slight but strong enough to carry Jane's weight. Together they left the bar. Belquassim and Paul and Bill watched them as they walked slowly down the beachfront road. It was getting dark. On the road, far above them, Belquassim noticed the newly erected billboard. A spotlight shone down on an advertisement for a brand of French, or American, cigarettes. The picture on the sign was of a tall beautiful blonde woman, an International Zone woman, a woman from nowhere. She was dressed in a fashion that Belquassim did not recognise and from her mouth issued a balloon. The French words in the balloon were, "You've come a long way, baby".

Paul noticed the sign as well. Noticed how the woman in the picture looked so large and strong, so material, so real, and noticed how ethereal and fragile Jane looked as she passed below it. He turned to Bill and said, "Sometimes I wish to God that I could come a long way. Let's go, it's late and I want to sleep."

VII

Sometimes I hate what I do and then I love it at the same time. I love the bantering with Bill. What I say is true at the time that I am speaking it. Then when I move outside of the moment I wonder if it really is true. But I suppose there is no real truth, it exists only at that moment, and its value at that moment is as real as its lack of value at another moment. Ideas change and truths change, this is I suppose their value. Paul never really engages in our bantering. Maybe it's because he has a fixed truth, a fixed value because he values nothing. Or maybe not, maybe it is because he is secure in the all-changing truths, which in the end equal nothing. I don't know.

And my body lusts after Cherifa. It is a horrible word, lust, it sounds so harsh, but I suppose lust is harsh. It knows no boundaries or rationality. Cherifa impales me. She is so dark, so wanton when we are together. I can't resist her. When she touches me it is as if she is putting a knife through my body, I can't move. I just get up and go when she calls. I sit on my knees in front of her, prayer-like, praying to the god of lust and passion. I reach out to touch her, and she pushes me away. Only she can touch, those long fingers, delicate on her rough market hands. Those long fingers over my nipples, squeezing them, fondling them. Watching my pleasure.

Obsession, obsessive. It's a feeling that so attracts me, but at the same time it repulses me. On the one hand I love the abandon of it all, the wildness, the danger. And Cherifa is dangerous. It's in her eyes, black-rimmed with pale irises. Paul is always telling me that all she wants is money and that she is trying to poison me. She gives me all these potions and necklaces, she says it's to help me stay healthy, but I know that she consults a sorcerer. In Morocco the concept of magic is so different. If I were in New York City I would laugh at what I have just said, black magic, a sorcerer. But here it has real meaning for me; people are always dying or getting sick because spells have been cast over them. And she has cast a spell over me, I cannot tear myself away from her.

When she touches me, and whispers to me, my body seems to have a life of its own. It just moves and responds and it refuses to be influenced by what I say in my head. I say don't stay, and I stay. I say don't tell her that you worship her, and I tell her that I worship her. There are no rules in this game of passion. And Paul, when Paul touches me, and when I touch him, my head and my hands move together. But when I touch Cherifa my hands move on their own, they have no guide. It's a kind of love I feel for her. But what is love really? I can't compare what I feel for her to what I feel for Paul, but can't they both be called love? Or, is love something that is reserved only for others? Something that I can never know?

༺༻

I am never sure if I like going to the bar with Bill and Jane or if I go just to pass the time. If I find Bill amusing, in his junkie way, it is because I admire his ability to pass the time this fucked-up way. And so I listen to him to find out more. Why am I thinking of passing the time? It could be that, now my book is complete, I need to think what else I can write so that I too can pass the time. I have time on my mind. Time and its continuing existence in life. What after all is life except trying to find ways to pass the time? Life can be amusing or interesting or even beautiful. But in the end, whether you enjoy what you are doing or whether you do not, it all amounts to finding a way to make time pass. If I believe in nothing, then this is what I must believe: life is making time pass by. If you believe in anything else you give it a meaning. And there is no meaning for me. The only thing that comes after time, is time.

Why am I digressing when all I was thinking was whether or not I enjoyed last evening at the bar? Oh yes, it is because Bill has found a perfect way to pass time. He sleeps and he takes junk. And then when he has a moment, because sleep and junk take up a lot of his time, he writes. Sometimes I wish I could take as much junk as he does. Well I don't even take junk, I just smoke kif, but sometimes I wish I could take it. Maybe it is my need to be in control. Kif does take me out of control and I like it, it inspires me to be out of control for that time. But I know that in a short while I will be back in control, it is not forever the kif feeling.

Maybe I am deceiving myself. Maybe I cannot be a junkie because something does mean something. Maybe my writing means something. The words, my writing, my thoughts that I create by clicking at the keys of my typewriter. I do believe in my writing, but I am not sure that I care about it. In the end it too means nothing.

My head jumps around. I think unlike how I write. Fragments of things are in my head. And I order the fragments, then make them cohere, and they flow. Then I control my thoughts. Control. I don't think about it often because I am in control. Sometimes I think about my childhood because that is a time when I was not in control. A child can necessarily not be in control – the parent or whoever looks after the child is in control. I am sure that my childhood was like the childhood of many others, controlled absolutely by my father. Maybe my response was exaggerated, but I respond badly to being controlled. Maybe my response is to write. In writing, unlike music, I have to think of the people in the story, I have to think of where my characters are and how they will respond to what they are doing. I control them. I don't judge them. What have I got to do with my characters? Nothing, they decide what to do although I write about it. But I leave myself out of their lives, I do not impose myself on their lives. I therefore cannot judge them. But I do control them.

Why does Jane drink so much? I am glad that she is able to pass the time by drinking but I am not glad that I have to look out for her safety when she is so drunk that she cannot stand. Do I care about Jane because I look out for her when the liquor intoxicates her?

VIII

The room was hot even though the door to the balcony was wide open. There was no wind, the sultry air was still. Paul sat cross-legged on the floor next to the small table. On the table was a half cup of coffee, an ashtray with a rolled kif cigarette in it and Jane's whisky glass. It was full. As soon as the liquid was finished Jane would fill the glass again. It never seemed to be empty. Jane moved all the time. Paul sat, he sat still, only his hands moved, sometimes to pick up the kif, sometimes to turn the pages of the manuscript which sat on his folded knees and sometimes to move his glasses. He wore glasses when he read. When he lowered his head the glasses were perched on his nose, when he raised his eyes to look up he held them and pointed to the page or to whom he spoke. His eyes and his hands were his only movement.

"I suppose I have to earn some money," Paul complained. "Who knows what will happen to my book, who knows if people will want to buy it?" He watched Jane as she poured another glass of whisky.

"Write," she said. "I can't seem to do it any more. Oh I do write … little scraps, and then I destroy them. But I can't write and earn anything. So you write … What is it you are writing this time?"

Paul held the manuscript up. "A review of this play by Sartre for the *New York Times*. It will open at the Biltmore in a few weeks, but it has already played to audiences in Paris. I wonder if I must review the English translation or the original French."

"Read it to me, read what you have written so that I can hear it," Jane said. "I know that a writer only wants praise, and I will give praise to you."

"*Huis Clos*," Paul continued, "*Huis Clos* … Yes, listen to this because they will not listen in New York … They will not listen because they will not understand. Do you think I had better write on *No Exit* or *Huis Clos*? The French words and the English words … Why do they mean something different even when they are supposed to mean the same thing?"

He looked up at Belquassim as he spoke. Now as a thought entered his mind he needed Belquassim to answer. "If I hear the stories of some of the Moroccan people in Moghrebi or Arabic and then I translate them for an American audience into English, do I impose my understanding on the language? I suppose I must do this, how can I do otherwise? The essence of the story is the same one, but they are my words, I choose them."

"I think that when I speak to you in English or French or Moghrebi," said Belquassim, "I say the same things, I understand them to be the same, and I think you understand them as they mean the same to me."

"Meaning, I wonder what it is," continued Paul, "maybe it is just the construction of this play that I like. It does not matter what the language is. The construction of the existentialism of this play: three people in a room with a Second Empire chair. It is not what Garcin, Inez and Estelle actually say, the room that these three people are in tells me what Sartre thinks hell is. Yes, even if the American audiences have never heard of this philosophy, the way the play is constructed will surely draw them into it."

There was a sound from down the stairs. It was a hard insistent sound, a knock on the downstairs door. Belquassim looked up; he looked at Jane, for it could only be Cherifa who would visit the house at this time. Jane looked into her whisky, "Be a darling," she said to Belquassim. "Run downstairs and let her in, she must have forgotten her key somewhere." Belquassim got up from the floor where he sat with his back to the wall. As he passed Jane she handed him her whisky glass, "And on the way back, please …" She smiled a dreamy smile, a smile that did not want to think about the play that Paul was writing about, although she listened to him. The smile that Belquassim knew she used to try to overcome whatever she thought was a difficulty. A smile that she used to help her through the night.

Belquassim walked down the stairs. He opened the door. Cherifa stood there, the long white man's *djellaba* trailed in the dust of the street. She wore a perfume tonight; the smell of musk was let into the doorway. Cherifa did not greet Belquassim, she walked past him and up the stairs. Belquassim followed her. She was not tall, but her white cloth *djellaba* filled the space between the walls as she walked. Her shadow on the stairs was larger than she was. She entered the room where Paul and Jane were sitting. She did not say anything. She walked up to Jane and showed her a small piece of paper. "Why is it not yet mine?" she asked, "you said it would be mine."

Jane looked at her. "It will only be yours once it becomes mine," she replied and looked over at Paul. "And when it is mine will be when Paul gives it to me."

Belquassim knew that Jane spoke about the house in which they were living. He knew that Jane had promised to transfer it into Cherifa's name. And Cherifa wanted this house to be hers, a safeguard. He knew that Paul had promised to give Jane the house so that she could do with it what she wanted. But he had not given it to her yet.

Cherifa sat down next to Jane. She put her fingers on Jane's thigh, she stroked the pale pink material that covered the skin. Her hand moved gently. Jane did not move now. She was feeling the touch of the hand on her thigh. Belquassim looked at the glass in his hand. He moved towards the kitchen and opened the cupboard where Jane kept her whisky. He poured the liquid into the glass and returned to Jane. He handed her the glass and she put out her hand to take it. Cherifa took her hand from Jane's thigh and took the glass instead. She drank from the glass and then gave it to Jane. The glass was now half full. Belquassim could see Jane's fingers through the yellow liquid that swirled in the glass. The nails looked as if they were flies trapped in amber. Flies trapped in the glass, fixed to the liquid.

Paul looked at Cherifa. Belquassim knew that Paul knew that Cherifa was evil. Belquassim was afraid of her. He knew that she used magical powers to get what it was that she wanted. As if Paul could see into Belquassim's head he said, "I wonder what happened to my beautiful blue parrot." The parrot had died a week ago. They both knew that Cherifa had put a spell on the parrot as it watched her, watching as if it knew whatever she did, wherever she was. Not wanting it to see her and what she did with Jane, she had killed the parrot with magic.

"Hmmm ..." Paul said, as though continuing the earlier conversation, "it is a play about how the creation of what is right and wrong has fascinated people. Since men have become gregarious they have wondered about definitions and rules. They have tried to formulate rules to control their own instincts. But I like the way that Sartre writes about these rules. How he articulates beautifully the feeling of threat. Rules, a threat to the natural instinct of man. And man's natural instinct is that of attaining pleasure." He looked at the manuscript. He picked up the pen that lay on the floor and wrote a few words on a sheet of paper on the table next to him. He pushed his glasses closer to his eyes. "I think I must write a short review – you know what people who read newspapers are like. They read so little, and when they do they want it short. Hmm ... The test that the individual creates for himself ... the testing of these rules ... how instinct can beat the rules ... Yes, that is what I will say, how men strive to beat the rules that they themselves create to try to keep their passion and their pleasure in harness. And then when the rules are overcome, the overwhelming guilt, the uneasiness, the hell which men create. And so they remain in this hell. Testing the rules, breaking them, that hovering sense of retribution. The play takes place in hell."

Belquassim looked at him. He did not understand what Paul spoke about, he just liked to listen. He enjoyed Paul's voice, and it was as if he were talking only to him. Sharing his thoughts on this philosophy.

Jane put her arm on Cherifa's shoulders. She leaned forward to kiss her but Cherifa moved her face away. Belquassim knew that she did not like to be touched, she preferred to touch. She touched Jane, Jane did not touch her. Cherifa once again picked up Jane's whisky glass. "I do not know what happened to that bird," she said, "but that bird was not a Moroccan bird. You brought it from somewhere else. It did not belong here in this Moroccan house."

"Yes," said Paul, "that bird should not have been here, it was a foreign bird. It was a stranger." As always Paul acquiesced, but he never agreed.

"Bill always calls me an existentialist," Paul now spoke to Belquassim, "I am not sure why he says this of me. I have never met Sartre, but I suppose I do like to read his philosophy. Every good playwright is always a philosopher. Ha … I suppose Sartre is a philosopher who just happens to be a good playwright. In this play he writes that 'Hell is other people', and other people are hell. But I am not sure that I want to agree with what he said later in his writings. He tried to say that our salvation is with each other as this is the only way we are free to experience and so to be. I am not sure that we cannot save ourselves alone, that is if we think that we need to be saved. I am not sure that the solidarity of others is a perspective that I concur with. It does not make me think that we are not, what did Sartre say we were, yes, 'a useless passion'. Matthieu said it, I remember, in one of Sartre's novels, in one of the trilogy. But I think that human beings are confined to a life of solitariness, which is why I like it in this city. Here I have no illusions about my solitariness, I am outside the social milieu, I am outside of that which is familiar. So my solitariness is reinforced."

Jane looked down at his white hair as he spoke. Cherifa looked at the piece of paper that she held and continued to move on Jane's thigh. Her hands moved. They move, thought Belquassim, as if she is casting a special sort of spell on Jane.

"I keep on thinking that there must be a meaning in it all," Jane said to Paul. "There must be something for me, there must be something that I search for, there must be something that I can put in my writing even if it is blackness."

"Your belief is so sentimental," said Paul. He did not look up from the pages that he read from. "Your belief is sentimental and it is therefore suspect." He put the pages on the table and picked up his kif. His blue eyes were hazy. "I have finished this now, maybe there will be a few dollars for us when they publish it."

He got up from the chair. He beckoned to Belquassim. "Come," Paul said, "let's listen to that music, I need to find money so that I can tape more music. Americans will not understand the music, but at least I must give it to them."

Belquassim got up from the floor. He followed Paul from the room. He closed the door behind him as he left the room. He knew that Jane would continue to sit where she was. He knew that Cherifa would move her hands over Jane's body and cast her spells. He knew that Paul knew this too. He knew that he had to leave the room of spells and follow Paul.

"I liked that blue parrot," said Paul.

IX

Tomorrow I must go to the post office and telex the review to the New York Times. *I need the money.*

Does Jane know that I translated the Sartre play into English? I am not sure that I told her this. It seems strange that I will review a play that once consisted only of French words put together by Sartre, but now consists of my words in English. Sartre constructed the play in French, he chose the words that he wanted to use. I remade it in English; I chose the words that I wanted to use. And I suppose I must review the English version of the play, my version, for that is what the Americans will see performed, this is what they will hear. And yet, while the ideas are Sartre's, the play is mine. The play in translation is my own. I like the construction of the play, but I am a stranger to some of its ideas. A world of nothing, the existentialist world where choice is the only explanation for men's actions. Actions, the only indication that there is less than nothing – yes, that I like. He does not say what is right or wrong, only that the rules we create are to inhibit us from just taking pleasure. And yet do we do this? What is pleasure? It is different for all of us. Sometimes pleasure for me requires a rule to be broken, at other times it does not. Have I harmed anyone with my pleasure? And if I have harmed them it is surely only because they themselves have their own rules that they believe I have broken – that is how I harm them.

I think sometimes that I am a stranger to pleasure.

Does Cherifa harm Jane? She killed the parrot, I know that. But I do not feel she has harmed me. The parrot is dead. I liked the parrot. But how can I judge her for what she did to that bird? She needed it dead, I did not need it alive, and maybe she needed it dead for a reason I cannot understand. But I cannot judge her. And yet I do not like Cherifa. I do not like her because I fear that she will harm Jane. I fear that she will hurt Jane. And I live through Jane, I look at her fear, and I feel it. And yet I can do nothing about Jane and Cherifa. I want to do nothing. I can only tell Jane what I believe, and even then she cannot believe me as she enjoys the fear that Cherifa builds up for her. It is almost as if she needs to go into this fear. She needs to enter into the fear so that she can feel it, she needs to enter into it to feel that she is alive. And I am outside life so I just stand and watch her.

I must give Jane the house.

§

I sit and listen to Paul talk about his writing. I sit and listen to what he has written. I know that all he wants from me is my praise, and I will give it to him. He knows that I can no longer write and yet he always tells me to write. He knows that my views on what he writes will not affect him or what he says and yet he asks me for my praise. I wish I could still write, write more than a small amount of words on little pieces of paper that I throw away. I wish that I could still ask Paul for his praise as once I did. I want to think with Paul. I want to remember with him.

Cherifa gave me a strange perfume tonight. It is a fragrance that I do not know. The fragrance of a princess. What was it like, this smell? A mixture of the blossom of the bitter orange tree mixed with rose oil and a little bit of musk. I wonder who made it for her or if she mixed it herself. Distilling and mixing the creation of a secret smell. A little bit of the orange tree added to the rose, the addition of musk to make it spicy, more exotic. I remember a man who worked in the perfumery for Chanel in Paris telling me about what a perfume needs. Rich top notes – here it is the orange blossom – then the heart of the scent, the musk. Sensuous. Was this perfume made especially for me I wonder? A gift for me. Cherifa … she is a dreamy smell, sweet like a child's caresses, the erotic movement of the bow over the strings of the violin, rich and corrupt. I want her magic.

I want her magic more than I want Paul's words. I want what her magic and her perfume will do for me. I want it forever now.

X

Jane and Belquassim sat on the narrow balcony of the house. She had been to New York City for a week and had recently returned. She was reading to him an extract from her novel.

"I can't live without her, not for a minute. I'd go completely to pieces."
To which one of her serious friends replies: "But you have gone to
pieces, or do I misjudge you dreadfully?" "True enough," says Mrs
Copperfield, "I have gone to pieces, which is a thing I have wanted to
do for years ... but I have my happiness, which I guard like a wolf,
and I have authority now and a certain amount of daring, which, if
you remember correctly, I never had before."

"And that's how I want to feel," said Jane to Belquassim. "I have gone to pieces. But I don't know if I have that certain amount of daring yet. I tell people that I have it and maybe they believe me, I don't know. Maybe because what I do, like walking alone in the *souk*s, loving Cherifa, drinking, makes them think that I have that daring. And I don't have authority, Paul has that. And I don't feel the happiness, just little bits of it now and again. That's why I think something explodes in my head and in my body, why I get sick so often. I try all the time to live by standards that I have set myself, values that I have created for myself. But not many people can understand this. They think that if your values are not theirs, then you must be crazy, or lonely, or sad. And then when they tell me that I must be crazy, lonely or sad, for a minute I think that I am, and then I really do go to pieces. And it's a never-ending circle. I want to go to pieces because then I think that too will bring me that daring, but when I do go to pieces it feels awful." She yawned and then continued, "I feel a bit like a pet monkey that has been brought to civilisation from the wild. Those New Yorkers, they all love me, they adore me, they pat me on the head and say, 'Jane darling, you are just so creative, you are so clever. How do you do it? It's so daring, you are such a success', but they never really think of me as a real person. They may think that I am daring, but they never take my autonomy from their normal dull world seriously. I am never a part of them. And sometimes, when it gets to me, when I feel insecure, then I think that I have made the wrong choices. Why did I choose Paul? Why am I not a wife and mother like all those ladies that I grew up with? It would make things so much easier. I would at least be a person, someone whom the world can recognise, just another person in a New York brownstone house." She leaned forward to reach for her glass on the table next to Belquassim. As she did so she took some time to look at him, then leaned over and stroked his hair, before picking up the glass. "It's why I drink. I hate it when people impose their meagreness on me. I have fallen into pieces, Mrs Copperfield and me. I want to feel what Mrs Copperfield feels." The liquid slipped from the glass, it made a small shadow on her yellow silk blouse, her red lipstick was smeared across her mouth. Belquassim thought she looked beautiful in the half-light of dusky Tangier. She seemed to take the city inside her in a way that he could not possibly do even though he had lived there all his life.

"I'm not sure that I understand you," Belquassim said, "but let me tell you about the women in Tangier. These women live a life behind a *haik*. It covers up their faces so that no-one can see them when they walk in the streets. And they wear perfume which is so beautiful that it's not they that attract you but their smell, that secret smell of orange blossom in the early morning. And who ever really knows them, there is a screen between them and the world? But when they get home, when they are with their girlfriends or their sisters, or their lovers, they take off their *haik*, they take off their perfume and they become people. These women laugh and scream and gossip and talk about the world. It is only at home that people know them." Belquassim brushed a stray eyelash from the corner of Jane's eye, there was a tenderness in his touch. He did not want the eyelash to get into her eye that was bright with the whisky because then his world would become a haze to her, it would be blurred and fuzzy. "You must learn to wear a *haik*, try not to want people to know you, except all of us at home. Don't care about New York's people, what do they really know? They should not know you, only a few of us should have that privilege ... Maybe this is a backward thought – but I know that it's not. How can it be, if when you take off your *haik* you are a person?"

The sun lowering reached down its tentacles, touching Jane's heart. "Love you," she said quietly, and took another sip of her drink. She leaned back into her chair and moved into some remote place of her own. The sounds of the street drifted upwards. A man selling dates and figs walked past the balcony below them on the road. His call reached up to them, "*Bzef ... Eemeek*". Suddenly Jane got up and grabbed Belquassim's hand. "Let's get some figs, we can have them after dinner tonight – they will be fresh and red and just perfect for dessert ... or we can eat them now. I love that sweet taste of fresh figs. Hurry, or he will disappear."

They ran inside from the balcony and down the stairs. Jane took some money off the sideboard as they passed through the hallway and they hurried laughing down the stairs to the street. The figs were cheap, fifty for ten pesetas, so they bought them all.

"And anyway he will never give us change," said Belquassim, "it's the way they cheat us."

Jane laughed again. "You do generalise, darling. Why do you Moroccans always say such disparaging things about yourselves? And anyway, so what if he cheats us? We all cheat someone at some time or another. And who are they? They are us."

"True," Belquassim replied, "but remember, we can't cheat each other. That would be cheating."

"I feel like a young boy," she called back. "Let's be daring, let's run away to the sea." And while they sat on the stairs in front of the house Belquassim knew that, for the moment, Jane had forgotten her melancholy. She looked like a painting sitting on the stairs ruthlessly eating her fig, tearing at its soft green skin with her short red nails to get at the pinkish fruit beneath it, crushing the flesh against her lips. She looked like a young boy, her small breasts barely visible beneath the silk of her sloppy yellow blouse that was now stained with the juice of the figs and whisky. The sound of the sea murmured through their voices.

A little later they went into the house. Jane smiled and took Belquassim's hand.

Cherifa was at home. Cherifa, dark-skinned and dreamy. Belquassim remembered Jane saying "Cherifa is one of the only women who has consistently evaded me. I can never seem to get her to really want me. Oh yes, she does want me, I can feel that she wants me, but her body is separate from anything else. Her body wants me, but her heart, that I cannot know. And there are all those other women in her life, ones I can never compete with, and in fact don't want to compete with as I am so different to them." Belquassim did not reply as he knew that whatever he said could not influence her. Instead he thought to himself of the stories that circulated in the *medina*, stories about the magical control Cherifa exerted over Jane, the gossip being that the only reason that she remained with Jane was for her money. Many a bargain had been struck between Jane and Cherifa about money. Money for Cherifa's house, promises of payments with nothing in return except long dark fingers and secret nights. He thought that Cherifa alienated Jane from the comfort and security of Paul. But he knew he would have to keep silent for Jane loved Cherifa. Not like he loved Paul. His feeling was so different from Jane's – he loved Paul, not just for sexual passion but for his mind and for what he could teach him.

It's probably where Mrs Copperfield comes from, thought Belquassim. Freedom through this strange kind of love. And at the same time he could not help but hope that Cherifa remained a part of Jane's life, no matter how dangerous she really was. If Cherifa stayed then there would be a place for him: he could take Jane's place next to Paul. Freedom for me through this strange kind of love, he thought. Space for me and my kind of love.

Cherifa shook her head at them. Wisps of her black hair lay across her face, oily and thick. Her voice was deep, it commanded Jane. "Come," she said. She had no need to say anything more. Then in Moghrebi she said to Belquassim: "You make her into a child, and you … this house is filled with children. Go away, there is no space for you now."

And as he drifted out onto the balcony again, Belquassim saw a small street boy squirm down the railings and run off down the street. "What a little thief!" he thought to himself as he leaned over to watch the child run away. He smiled to think that not so long ago he too had been a thief. But those times were past. He had Paul now, he did not need to be a thief.

By now it was getting dark. The sound of the mosque reverberated in the distance. The smell of hashish and figs penetrated his nostrils. A man called out to his wife or children from somewhere in the *medina*. Belquassim heard Jane and Cherifa in the top bedroom. He heard the door close and the portable radio that Jane kept on the table next to the bed being turned on. Jane's perfume reached down and moved through the narrow staircase. Then it settled somewhere near him. He thought he heard her laugh, lightly in the dusk. And then laughter and passion mixed into a single whispered sound. In a while, he thought, I must go and make them some coffee.

XI

I often wonder why Jane is so preoccupied with the views of others? Now
that she has returned from New York she is full of "so and so said this",
or "so and so said that". All that kind of talk. She is so concerned about
what they think of her that it paralyses her and she can no longer write.
It is because they, whoever they are, may not like her writing, they may
not appreciate it or her. As it is, the New Yorkers do not really like her
book, or her play for that matter, and it crushes her.

She always talks about judgement. "Why do they judge me?" She
even thinks that I judge her, since I always try to tell her to write more.
I hate judgement. I do not judge and I do not care if anyone sits in
judgement on me. No, maybe that is not entirely true. I do judge the
stupid and the prosaic. But then I avoid this kind of person or thing
and move away so that I no longer have to judge.

And Jane. I do not judge Jane. Just sometimes I wish she would
not get so anxious, it gets on my nerves, it irritates me. I suppose she
has to create her own suffering, and all suffering in Americans must
come from neurosis. They have nothing else to suffer about. I am not
neurotic so I do not suffer.

Maybe I will go into the medina and buy Jane a haik so that
she can walk the New York streets and not be seen. Maybe then her
neurosis about judgement will go away.

Judgement and suffering bore me."

৽

I was sitting on the balcony last night, Cherifa had gone home, gone
off to her other women I suppose, Paul and Belquassim had gone to
bed. It was late, maybe it was even early morning, I can't seem to tell
what time it is any more. And then I saw the moon. It was a thin sliver

of silver in the sky, riding up and over the harbour and the lighted ships that are moored there. It was as thin as a woman's wrist. But then as I looked harder I could see its whole shape, its full size. The glazed edges of the whole enveloped the bright silver sliver. It was a new moon, but it was engulfed by the old. It could not escape what it was, its shadow will always be there.

I went inside to get a silver coin. I put it in my pocket and turned it round and round. Mother always said that if I saw a new moon I should turn my money over in my pocket, and this, one day, would make me rich. But will it work this time if I can also see the old moon? Mother always comes up with these Jewish things, I am so far away from being Jewish nowadays. There are few Jews in Tangier. And this is my home now. Mother and her Jewishness is a home that I have long ago moved out of, moved far away from. Am I one of the dispossessed now? Part of a different diaspora, a diaspora of choice. And I am so comfortable in Tangier, a place where difference matters little and everyone is assimilated. Yet the Jews were driven out of Morocco, out of this city, killed for being Jewish. Yesterday I went to visit the Jewish cemetery in the centre of the city. It is a desolate place, the stones that have been put next to the graves seem to have been put there a long time ago. I suppose that is why Jews put stones next to a grave, they last, whereas flowers do not. And yet for some reason I wanted the graves to be covered in flowers. It was almost as if the flowers signify a former sense of happiness. But there were none, there were no flowers, there were only stones. A little old shrunken man then came in to the cemetery. He saw me and started talking. It was almost as if he had found a kindred spirit, someone else who was Jewish in this town. He didn't know that I am no longer Jewish, I have left that behind me, behind me somewhere in the vast obscure vistas of my childhood. I am not there any more. Maybe one day I will embrace Mary, the Mother of God. Why not, I embrace women anyway, so why not her? And she is so beautiful in her blue dress.

Someone said – who it was I can't remember – that dispossession became the condition of his art. Now that I am dispossessed I cannot write. Maybe I wrote when I was in the thick of a life and values that I hated. I wrote about hating it and getting away from it all. Now that I am outside of that I cannot write. Possession is the condition of my art.

I miss Mother sometimes.

XII

Paul had, after much correspondence with those who seemed to be influential persons in Washington and New York, received a grant from the Rockefeller Foundation to record the indigenous music of Morocco for the Library of Congress. He wanted to record it so that the world could hear a new sound, foreign sounds, sounds that their ears had never heard. For the next few weeks Belquassim travelled with Paul, from village to village, through the desert and through the mountains, recording the music of men and women, religious music, music for festivals, lullabies and party songs.

The day before they left Tangier the small house was filled with boxes and packages for the journey: recording equipment, coils of cable and boxes of tapes. A trunk of clothing, for it was cold in some parts, and Paul's typewriter. "Just how long do you think you are going for?" Jane asked. "It looks as if you will never come back, there is a whole lifetime in these boxes."

"A short lifetime," Paul replied looking at the boxes, "I need much more than this for my life, which I suspect, and probably unfortunately, will be a long one."

Belquassim helped Paul pack the small car, recording equipment on the back seat so that it would not get damaged, long pieces of cloth between the machinery to insulate it from the bumps on the rough and stony road. They got into the car, Paul behind the wheel. Belquassim did not know how to drive a motor vehicle, this travelling machine. Jane leaned into the front window, and kissed Paul, twice, once on each cheek, before they left. And as they drove out of the courtyard and into the narrow street outside, Belquassim turned back to look at her. A slight dark figure set against the white of the house.

She raised her arm, brought the fingers of her right hand to her lips and kissed them, then lightly blew the kiss in the direction of the moving car. But the wind caught this kiss and moved it sideways so that it did not reach them. It floated off over the flat roofs of the houses and then pushed out and over the sea. It probably travelled to Spain.

It was still dark when they left, the dusky dark of the early morning. The dawn chorus of roosters and sparrows and other inhabitants of the city called to them as they navigated the narrow streets. At the outer edges of the city the squalid shacks of the poor greeted them. The poor who no longer lived in either the city or the rural districts, but who were doomed to live out their lives on the outer edges of nowhere. The outer edges of the International Zone where they had no place or space or culture. Somewhere in this array of shanties Belquassim knew that his mother lived, but he could no longer remember exactly where the house was. He knew that if asked to point out the house he would no longer be able to do so. He often wondered why he no longer went to see her. Maybe it was because he just wanted to remember her when she was young, beautiful and hopeful, not as she was now, bitter and wrinkled.

By the time the sun rose, yellow against black, they were far away from Tangier. They did not speak to each other. There was no need to communicate, the landscape was enough to fill the space that sat between them on the red leather seat of the car. Belquassim smiled, he was alone with Paul.

The journey to Taza took several hours. They drove through the valley between the Middle Atlas and the Rif Mountains. The mountains, seeming bigger than they could ever be, surrounded them on either side in their small moving vehicle. There were no sounds on this road. They passed the mangled body of an ape that lay spread out on the road. A troop of monkeys sat beside it, watching death and what it did to the living. They seemed perturbed, but curious.

They did not stop, but now and again Belquassim would pour hot coffee from the thermos that Jane had prepared and hand it to Paul. The steam from the coffee hit the cold air and melted above Paul's head as he took long deep sips of the black thick liquid. Once they stopped for the sweet mint tea that was sold at roadside cafés along the way. It was cold. They were accompanied only by the shadows. Shadows of death and insurrection. Paul talked constantly about the war, the vilification of Europe. But as he spoke Belquassim could hear that his thoughts were not in Europe, his concern was not Europe or the people that lived there, but the images that Europe created for him.

"Power," Paul said, "is a strange thing. It cannot be analysed by those who do not understand it, and the big problem is that only those that have it really understand it. They understand the strength and power of power." It was almost as if he spoke to himself. Belquassim was just a sounding board, the hollow drum into which the variety of notes that made up Paul's voice disappeared.

"A man who wrote in French words said that it was in the Spanish Civil War that men learnt that you can be right and still be beaten. They suddenly saw that there are times when courage is not a sufficient reward for your endeavours. I was not there, but I know many that were. Many who died with their Barcelona comrades. And the ones who are alive, now, twenty years after that futile struggle, so many of them still think upon this war as their own personal tragedy. They lost more than a struggle for equality and integrity, they lost themselves." Paul just spoke. At times Belquassim could understand what he was trying to tell him, at other times he could not be certain what he meant. Occasionally Paul spoke about Jane. She had recently been ill. It was after her return from New York. She had been depressed and was drinking more than before. And she was not writing. Belquassim thought that Paul must be worried, but that he would not admit this. Was he wrong? Did Paul really worry, or was he just speaking about Jane not out of concern but because he enjoyed the sound of his own thoughts. When he spoke of Jane it was about her writing, their travels to other parts of the world, Mexico, the parrot they had owned in Mexico City, the circle of friends who visited them.

Paul had tried to postpone the journey. Did this show worry?

But both he and Jane knew that time for the project was running out. The first recordings had to be sent to Washington in only a few months. And both of them also knew that Paul was restless, he needed to move somewhere. So Jane had insisted that they take the trip to the mountains. "Go, go," she had said to Paul, "you must get away from this hustling city with its acerbic expatriates and its winding claustrophobic streets. You need the outside. I will be fine, you know that I will be fine – how can I not be? – I will be here when you return. And anyway you must spend the money that those generous Americans have given you. Just leave a little behind for me. You would not be happy to know that I died of thirst while you were away." Jane spoke as if she knew Paul did care. Maybe she needed to persuade herself, maybe she was right.

But Belquassim worried – if Jane was not there, what then? He remembered Paul saying earlier, "If she is gone the only emotions that I know will go with her. What will I do with the rest of my life?"

It was a Sunday, and it was Belquassim's birthday.

As they drove further the road became narrower, in certain parts two vehicles could not pass each other for fear of falling off the cliffs that perilously lined them. Here and there a goat wandered. Paul stopped the car on the side of the road near a café and they both got out and looked out over the snow-hedged mountains. "He is holding the world on his shoulders, Atlas that is," said Paul to Belquassim. "It's a tiring job: imagine keeping the world afloat." And then he laughed. "Imagine the size of his shoulders," he said. The mountains were beautiful, in fact as Belquassim looked out along the curve of the plateau, and watched Paul point his hand northwards, he knew the value of words. Paul's words. "The world could never have been created in an explosion," Paul said. "It must have been slowly created by a writer who knew how to put passion into words." He spoke again, this time more softly, "But I can't find the words to create them. These mountains, they have their own beauty, yet, for me, they can have no meaning without words. I must put them into words or they will cease to exist."

Belquassim knew that for him this memory would remain forever etched in his mind. A picture of Paul standing on the edge of the mountain, cigarette in hand, the smoke cutting brightly up through the stark white peaks, rubbing his balls and laughing. Maybe Paul's questions were right; words could not describe this beauty. But a face will always be a picture. A picture can describe these mountains, thought Belquassim. And I will always picture this face against these mountains. He wondered why he was the only one who could see them clearly.

Together they walked down to the nearby café. The smell of mint tea and hashish assailed them as they entered. A chained monkey sat on one side of the room and a chained eagle perched on a stick was at the other. A black and white dog lay in the corner of the café mauling a bone that had no meat on it, it was picked clean white. Paul asked the proprietor for tea and they drank it. While they sat Belquassim told Paul the story of his grandfather. His grandfather, whom he had scarcely known, was a trader. His mother would always tell Belquassim the story that twice a year his grandfather would gather jewellery that he had bought from village families and walk for more than forty-five days to Fes, Meknes and Rabat, through these same mountains, to sell the jewellery in the *souk*s. Jewellery that had been with people for centuries. Where was it now, Belquassim wondered? He remembered his grandfather. He was an old man who never took off his *djellaba*, whatever the weather. He knew no French, or if he did he had purposefully forgotten it. He told stories in murmured Moghrebi to all his grandchildren. They would sit at his feet, or in his lap. His grey and white beard would prick the soft skin on their dark faces, or if they sat at his feet he would rest his tired hand on coal black heads, soft hair under work-stained fingers.

The stories were of a time before foreigners, before the wars in Europe, which drove the expatriates into Tangier, before the division of the country. Stories of a time that was foreign to Belquassim. They were stories that had been told many times. Stories that were told not only by his grandfather, but by all the old men of Morocco. Stories of perfumed nights and blue turbaned illusions. Stories of dark and fierce camel riders who would drive the animals hard by beating them with thick sticks or pricking them behind their ears with sharp silver forks. These men in blue or white or black would ride their camels for long periods and they would not drink. The camels did not need water, and so they believed they did not need it either. And at night, in the cold, they would sit next to the bodies of camel heat and draw the path of the stars so that they would know the direction that they would have to take the following day. Sometimes his grandfather would pull his grandchildren closer to him and read from the Holy Book. Stories of the Prophet Mohammed. How, with a stone tablet in his hand, he would show the people where the words of God were written. The Prophet would tell the people of heaven and what life on this earth meant for all men. It meant nothing. Being on this earth was a prelude, a period of work, before they could find their place in heaven. A place where there was no concern as there was nothing that anyone needed to be concerned about. The writing in the Holy Book was curved like the scimitar that was used by the Prophet in the wars against the infidels. "Never get close to a Nazarene," his grandfather would whisper to him and the other children, "they can give you nothing, not even dreams, nothing ..."

No-one served them with food so Paul went up to the counter to choose some of it. The table they sat at was stained with the food and drink of others who had been there before them. A broken-edged heart with a name written inside it was carved into the wood. Paul approached the counter to search the many dishes in their steamy hot tubs. Small cockroaches scuttled along the rim of the tubs and occasionally raised their heads and looked out. Then they would run hungrily back into the tubs and make off with a scrap of something. When he returned with their food and sat down he said, "Have I shown you that painting by Bruegel? I have the postcard at the house. It's the one with Icarus falling out of the sky. His wax wings have melted in the sun, and down below people are going around conducting their business without a thought for the poor, almost dead boy. The cockroaches remind me of this painting. It's like a miniature Bruegel: they are running back and forth over the tubs, watching the world, and yet its tragedies continue around them and they don't give a damn." Paul's white hair hung down over the upturned collar of his thick lambswool jacket, the stew was also lamb. Hungrily they ate. Paul raised his glass of tea, "Happy birthday!" he said smiling, and Belquassim turned twenty.

In the left hand corner of the café next to the chained monkey sat two men, they were rough-looking, not country people but from a city, moving for some purpose through the mountains. In Moghrebi Belquassim heard one say to the other, "arse fuck-ing foreigner and his sell-out whore". The other man glanced in their direction and made a crude gesture with his thumb and forefinger. Then he got up and walked towards them. The chained gold eagle let out a cry that hovered in the air above the room. The monkey laughed excitedly. Belquassim got up slowly; he wanted to leave. As the man got close to them he took a knife out of his pocket, as sharp as a snake's tongue. The monkey stopped his laugh. The eagle became still. The man was tall. He leaned over Belquassim. Belquassim could feel his hot breath on his skin, it smelled of boiled eggs. Slowly the man drew a line with the silver sliver of metal across Belquassim's face. The sound of moving flesh rattled in Belquassim's ears, it was slow and rasping. The knife moved down across his eye and over his mouth. There was no sound except the laughter of the blade. In the silence the monkey and the eagle watched the charade. The man then went back to where he was sitting and continued to drink his tea. The blood dripped across the table, it filled the cracks of the name in the carved-out heart and then fell to the floor. "Drip drip drip." It was like rain, red rain, nourishing the cold stone floor. Belquassim could do nothing, he was paralysed. The dog in the corner looked up at this violation. Then it walked over to the pool of blood that lay on the floor next to the table, and licked at the scarlet liquid, tentatively at first as if to taste it. It seemed to like the taste of human suffering. Its muzzle was soon covered in red, it slobbered and slavered as it went "lick lick lick". It reminded Belquassim of a story told to him by Paul. The story of Dracula, the count who lived forever only to see the moon and to suck out the blood of beauty. Yes, he was Count Dracula's victim, maybe now he would live forever. He did not react, he could not react, almost unconsciously, he pulled a piece of cloth from his pocket and held it to his face to try and stop the bleeding. Paul got up from the chair. He said nothing. Belquassim could see fear in his shaking fingers as he put twenty pesetas on the table and took Belquassim's arm. They left the room. The monkey pulled at its chain, jumping up and down, moving.

Outside Belquassim leaned down into the snow, grasped some in his hands and smeared it on his face. The liquid water and the liquid blood … he was drowning. Paul took the cloth and pressed it hard onto his face. Minute by minute the blood seemed to stop flowing. Now it only glazed his hand when he held it up to his face. They got back into the car. A small dirty child ran up to the window calling "un peseta, un peseta" but they paid no heed. How could they? The Moroccan landscape turned from white to brown in an instant. Was he the foreigner now? he thought to himself. His hands trembled.

They checked into a hotel just outside Taza. It was empty save for some ragged children and an old man who had been left in charge while the regular owner spent the winter in Marrakech. The old man helped them with the luggage and brought a pail of water for them to wash in. Belquassim wanted to rest. His face felt as if it was on fire. Paul gently touched his hair. "Stay here for a while. I will go down into the village and try to arrange for a guide to take us up into the mountains." Belquassim lay back on the hard narrow bed and closed his eyes. It was not yet dark. Some time later when the shadows were long Paul returned. He held a kerosene lamp in his hand, it smoked. He had procured the services of a guide. Anselmo would take them up to the top of the highest mountain peak and bring them back. After that they would go and look for the musicians.

The long unhealed scar ran from the corner of his right eye

to the corner of his mouth. It was a surface wound, nothing was really damaged. Gently Paul said to Belquassim, "The scar makes you look like a bandit. Maybe in the future when we stop at wayside cafés you will scare people, they will fear you now. You may even have a little power." Belquassim remembered his grandfather who would rub salt in his cuts so that they would heal quickly. The old man, as he served them food in the hotel dining room, looked at him as if he were a stranger.

Walking in the Atlas was tiring. By now they had reached the Orikano Valley. It had been two days since his birthday. Although it was winter it was hot in the valley. The sun seemed to reach over the high peaks that surrounded them. It poured across them, moving slowly into noon. The sheer sides of the mountains made climbing difficult. As they gained height so it got colder. Belquassim touched his own fingers, they were stiff with the cold. He called out to Paul, "Let's rest, I want to warm myself."

Anselmo moved higher up, looking out beyond the peaks to somewhere he would never be able to go to. Belquassim moved Paul's hands over his groin. He rose as high as the sun, he felt warmer, Paul's hands moved faster, Belquassim directed them, moving them, reminding him that he could, if he chose, always be warm. His passion rose inside him slowly, he quietly gave way to it pulling Paul roughly towards him. It was not passion any more, it was lust, the lust for warmth. His heart beat faster. Then at last the heated cream fell in droplets down Paul's fingers. Paul moved his hands over Belquassim's hair and down the new scar, "Emma Bovary was also called a whore in her time and she is one of the greatest creations in modern literature. Sometimes I think we should all live as if we were in a novel, then it would not hurt so much." Maybe we do live in a novel, Belquassim thought. But this is a story that I could never have imagined.

Paul called Anselmo and they resumed their journey. By now they were so high that Paul was finding breathing difficult. Below them, in the ochre houses that were carved into the sides of the mountain, and amongst the perfectly lined up olive trees that edged the escarpment, people carried on with living. Nature did not move on the mountain, only mythology and the two of them remained. At the top of the mountain they drank tea, sweet and sticky.

The following day they drove out towards the Rif Valley. "This is where the gods divided the land," Paul told Belquassim. "I forget who it was, one of them anyway, maybe it was Hercules, forged a way through the mountains to make this valley. And now, because we think that we are god we have divided the land too." The Rif was a dangerous place. Since the division of the country between the French and the Spanish, and the creation of the International Zone there had been famine in the area. Many drug smugglers and thieves roamed the lonely roads. They had been warned about travelling this route. Stories abounded about how the smugglers would rob travellers as they drove through. They were told that a favourite trick of the bandits was to lay a log across the road so that the car had to stop. Once someone got out to move the log the car would be surrounded. Guns and knives would be held to white necks. Travellers had lost everything on these roads.

The area was stark, not as mountainous, but harsh. Now and again there would be a small brown bush and the trees that lined the escarpment were like skeletons rattling their bones in the dry wind. Belquassim crossed his arms and held himself close. I hope that we are safe, he thought. He looked across at Paul who was driving. A bead of perspiration rolled down Paul's forehead. Then it fell. It dropped onto his white shirt and left a stain where it landed. It was hot in the car despite the cold wind that blew outside. Belquassim took out a cloth and wiped the stain away. "I'm tired," Paul said, as if in answer to a question that Belquassim had not asked. "All this moving to nowhere, and at the end a few musicians whom only I will appreciate and admire. And I am taping their music for a world that does not even know who they are, let alone who wants to hear and understand their music. But I feel especially tired because I think that I have reached the point where there is no turning back. I wonder why it has just come to me now. I suppose it is because despite feeling tired, despite the hard beds and bed bugs, despite everything, I feel as if I am at home just moving. I don't have to have a house with animals and a clean kitchen and furniture. I am at home moving." Belquassim looked at Paul, his eyes were bright as he spoke. "It was early in the morning, when you were asleep, I thought about the last line of my book, the one that I began in the desert. I thought about it as I looked outside the window of the hotel and saw the bus move down the street, it was filled with people, I do not know where they were going to, perhaps nowhere, maybe they were just there for the ride. Now I know that this line was right." And then Paul recited the line as if to confirm his thoughts. "'At the edge of the Arab quarter the car, still loaded with people, made a wide U-turn and stopped; it was the end of the line.' A perfect sentence for the book. A description of a line."

A while later they arrived in Chefchaouen – Chefchaouen, with its blue-walled houses and its streets that were covered with carpets, carpets for sale, carpets for decoration, red and orange carpets covering small holes in the walls to keep out the wind and the rain, the colours encroached upon only by thin black lines. The blue walls were built around small gardens with ponds in them. If you leaned over a wall, you could see the plants and the reflection of children distorted by the shadows of the walls. Belquassim and Paul walked lingeringly together down a narrow street. Belquassim leaned over one of the walls, his arms encircling Paul's waist, and together they watched the lively play. Touches of powder came off on his hands, they glistened. Through a blue doorway an old man rocked his child. He was singing a Moghrebi lullaby. The tiles over the house floor were also blue. Belquassim longed to go into one of these blue houses and just sit. He wanted to hold Paul, to comfort him, but he did not know why. And he knew that Paul did not want his comforting. He did not need it.

The musicians were ready, the café was decorated especially for the occasion, cloths covered the walls, striped bright in the hazy light. A group of men were to play the *rhaita*, a large oboe-like instrument that was designed for long distance listening, it was not an indoor instrument. After much difficulty with the batteries for the recording equipment Paul decided that the music should be recorded outside in the square. He was certain the enclosing walls of the small café would prevent the musicians from truly creating that jagged strident haunted sound that he loved. Once in the square the musicians immediately began. There were two *rhaita*, one played by an old man who looked as if he did not have sufficient air in his body to create the sound, the other by – strange for this area – a young woman. As the music began, so the crowds began to gather, soon there was a whole party going on around and in the square. Men and women, having escaped the strict Arab influence, danced together, young girls improvised with songs, and the *rhaita* played on. For several hours the revelry continued, at about three in the morning Paul suggested to one of the musicians that it was time they stopped. "But we are going on until tomorrow," he said, and so the party did. As Belquassim helped Paul to pack up the equipment the sounds of the music grew louder. It lit up the sky with notes as if smiling up at the cold moving clouds.

The next day Belquassim and Paul explored the town. The party was over, the musicians had gone home, it was peaceful, the smell of hashish and coffee on every corner. Old men, young boys, Spanish tourists disguised as Spanish gypsies came to smell the smells and to see the turquoise walls. Children ran in the narrow streets, while from behind the walls of the houses you could hear the sound of women's voices as they spoke melodically to families and laid out tables. The illusionary delights of another world, there for them, there for both of them. And soon it was time to leave. The next town, the next musicians.

XIII

The solitude of the desert and the solitude of the mountains. They are so different; the desert reintegrates the soul into the body so that nothing else is necessary for survival. The mountains engulf a person, they seem to create the need for closeness, the closeness of another person. It is not because a person is lonely that he needs another, but because the mountains crush down, they push you together, and then once you are there you cannot move out of being so close. But this can never be forever. It's momentary, it's like a tear. You feel the tear on the skin of your face, and then it moves downwards, pulled by forces outside your control, and drops away. No matter how many tears there are they will always drop, to the floor maybe. Transitory, like life, like love, like closeness. And what is the soul anyway? I do not cry ever. I wonder why I am thinking about tears?

A strange and horrible thing happened on the journey. I suppose this kind of thing must be expected wherever one is – strange and horrible, even when one thinks that one is outside of it. Belquassim and I were sitting in one of the roadside cafés when a man came over to us. He had a knife or some kind of blade in his right hand. I suppose he held it in the right hand as he felt he was doing a righteous thing, or maybe he was just right-handed. He said something to Belquassim. My knowledge of Moghrebi is not yet proficient so I could not catch precisely what he said, but it was something to do with being a whore. Then he used the knife to carve a thin line down Belquassim's face. Just once, one cut down the side of that pretty young face. I watched as if I was watching someone take a photograph, only a second, almost like the camera flash going off when a photograph is taken in the dark. And there was the blood. I know that the head, and the face particularly, bleeds a lot when it is cut, as the blood vessels are close to the surface, so I was not worried about the amount of blood. But

I could almost smell the fear. It cut through the room and smashed against me. I almost felt that I was the one who had been cut. I felt as if I was being pushed up against a wall, being sucked up and into a vortex and then pressed down upon by a weight, the dead weight of fear. And then it was over. There was only blood on the floor, once again, transitory, like the tear, like love, like a life.

We left quickly. Belquassim was in shock. I stopped the bleeding as fast as I could. It left a stain on my shirt and my handkerchief. It's the stain that will last, not the blood. How do I describe the emotion of fear? Is it the smell, or could I see it? It was tangible. It was there in the room.

And then there were a chained monkey and a chained eagle that looked on. I wonder what their thoughts were as they saw the blood fall and smelled the fear. Or did they just think about their own caged condition, their own fear, their own loss of freedom? I wonder if animals are sentient beings? I eat them, I have them in my house. But do they feel emotion? In that café the eagle uttered a cry that seemed to rend the air as if it knew what it witnessed, and the monkey laughed, laughter for the dead I suppose. But they looked as if they felt the fear. And now it is gone, the feelings of that day and I am getting along with the project at hand.

Recording this music is something that I have wanted to do for a long time, and I am enjoying it. And when it is released the recordings will give the country a voice, something that they have never had in my world. But will I be the only person who understands this voice in the tinsel rooms of New York? And even I, do I really understand, can I understand it?

∽

They take our country. They take our culture. They take our women. And now they take our boys. They take what it is to be a man from this country and they leave only sickly women behind. The cutting. I did that because violence makes me a man. I cannot drive them out but I can be a man. A man who can make blood flow. A man who is not a woman. They cannot take me. They cannot make me a woman. I must stay a man, stay a man because then I can do violence. I like *the sound of the blood. I like the feel of the knife. I like the smell of burning meat.*

෴

I like being with myself. I like the fantasy of being a woman expatriate in Tangier. Walking the souks. *Sitting in the bars. Drinking the whisky. I like the fantasy of being the solitary writer even though I no longer write. But that fantasy somehow gets lost when I sit before my typewriter. I am empty, no sound comes from the keys. But still I can think of me as the solitary writer. But that is a fantasy, so instead I hold on to others whom I do not know.*

I feel lonely with Paul away. I wonder why. It is not as if I am with him all the time when he is here. But it is, I suppose, just his presence that means so much to me. That incomprehensible closeness that we have, it is not a logical closeness, but it is one that I do not question. That is how I love him. But I suppose I encouraged him to go to the mountains, he wanted to get out of the city so much.

I feel lonely today without Paul here."

XIV

The three of them, Paul, Belquassim and Jane were in the Café de Paris. They were there to watch a film. The Café de Paris, which was something of an expatriates' club, all day long showed newsreels from America and Europe. Sometimes they showed a feature film. This evening it was a war film. Black and white images of the bathos. The Café de Paris was not like the bar at the Hotel Mirador. It had the pretence of seriousness, as a place where people gathered to discuss politics and the refurbishment of Europe.

"I will not judge or be judged, but sometimes I find it so difficult to maintain this position, judgement is so easy, it is so reassuring," Paul said to Belquassim. They were sitting on the balcony of the house waiting for Jane. "For instance, I sometimes find these kinds of evenings insufferable. These European conversations, they appear to be so decollated, so insubstantial. And yet they are not that for those that speak them. I feel like an outsider. Sometimes my mind manufactures its own adventures, and then I am not sure where reality is, outside in the European conversations, or inside, in my own adventures."

Belquassim watched Paul as he spoke. There was a haunting dead tone in his voice, and his eyes were fastened on something far away. "My thoughts, I suppose, are not comforting, to anyone …" he looked up at Belquassim "… especially not to those I care about, Jane most especially. But I can't reject my ideas. I must, at all costs, if I am to stay alive, keep something outside of me and beyond life. In a way I have to keep Europe outside of myself, and I can by being away from it."

"What happens if others can't remain outside of life as

you try to do, if they aren't able to create their own worlds?" asked Belquassim. He asked this question, not only because he was curious about Paul's thoughts, but also because he felt so immersed in life, he could not be outside it.

"I don't know," replied Paul, as he cupped his hands over a small flame to light a cigarette, "I suppose they will live their lives in the way that is most comfortable to them. But I, I must live in my own thoughts, I must see things and capture them through my own eyes. For instance, when I write about what I see, like stories of a street boy, I put these thoughts and stories down on paper, and the words, the words, they reflect what I see, my reality, or at least the reality that I create for him. The boys do exactly the same thing every day. They steal, they fuck and they starve. But how I put the words down is a different experience from their experience. It's not what they, or I, are saying, but how it is said. There is no truth, neither mine, nor theirs." The dusty breeze blew in from the harbour and mingled with the smoke that curled from the cigarette that Paul held between two fingers. In the summer the dust was sometimes so heavy. But not tonight, tonight there was just a light breeze, and a little dust.

The Café de Paris was showing an old movie. "However," Jane had told Belquassim earlier, "it may be old, but for its time it was considered risqué. It's about girls and their preferences, with a bit of fascism thrown in on top." She licked the index finger of her right hand and smoothed her left eyebrow.

"What I know about fascism is that it causes destruction," said Belquassim. He felt angry. What did she know about violence and oppression, what did she know about the French or the Spanish in Africa? What did she really know about the conquest of others' lives? "What about Hitler, the French colonists here in Morocco? I can't laugh at that disrespect for, and cruelty to, other people. Making people less than animals. How can it be fun or interesting?" He felt his voice rise, he was shouting.

Jane looked at him, her smile was wide, but her eyes had no colour in them as she said, "Ah, but that is where you are wrong darling, this is fantasy." And then her mood seemed to change as she traced the line of the scar on his face with her long fingers, "Don't you sometimes fantasise about a jackboot and a uniform, and a daddy? It's not real, you don't play out your fascist fantasies." Jane's voice was light-hearted, then it sank into being tired. "Maybe you do, how would I know? Fascist fantasies, maybe you live them? Maybe you too have been compromised." And then once again her tone changed. Now it had a smile in it. "Anyway it's called *Maidens in Uniform* and it should be quite sexy, girls in uniform. And you never know who we may meet there. I can't stand being with Cherifa at the moment. She wants to overpower me. And just the other morning she was telling me she wanted to replace all her teeth with gold ones. Can you believe it? Gold teeth, I can't bear it. And I can't bear it when she suffocates me like she is doing at the moment, I can't bear her rules. But I also can't bear to be without her." Belquassim did not reply. "Maybe," Jane continued, "I must do without her, maybe I'll meet someone tonight. Then her spell over me will be broken."

"Her spell," said Belquassim, "will never be broken. How can it be? If you love someone, then no matter what, you will love her forever."

"I will never love anyone forever," said Jane, "except Paul, because he is, he is who I love, he will always be there for me no matter what. I hate rules, but I like the rules he makes for me, they show me somehow that he cares even though he says he doesn't." Then she laughed as she mimicked Paul, "'Now no more whisky Jane, you are drunk. Enough of those cigars – they will kill you.'"

Jane linked her arm into Paul's as they walked down to the beach where the café was. It was full. The sounds of talk and music echoed brazenly among the ornate tables and people. Most of the people there were women. Emerald green scarves, brilliant red nails and lips curved into smiles, shining eyes and silver cigarette holders. "They all look like they have just stepped out of the pages of *Vogue* magazine," said Jane to Paul and Belquassim. "What fun we are going to have." They found a table in the corner of the room, close to one of the long windows that were open down to the floor. Jane continued to look around her excitedly. Paul looked out to sea where the green light of a fishing boat seemed to merge with the silhouette of the Spanish mountains. And Belquassim looked at both of them.

They ordered drinks from the tall Moroccan boy who came to their table, whisky for Jane and Paul, Coke for Belquassim. Behind the boy stood a woman, or maybe a girl. She was completely covered in a long black *djellaba*, over her face was a veil. She seemed to be following the boy's every movement. Because she was covered up you could not tell if she was old or young, ugly or beautiful. Paul turned to the boy and half to the woman, and said, "I thought women could not come into places like this. Surely her husband or brother doesn't allow it."

The woman did not reply, the boy seemed embarrassed: "I am teaching her how to wait at tables. Next time she will take the orders on her own. We are poor outside this café, we all need to work. Even our religion must disappear for money. And anyway, I am here to look after her. She is my younger sister, I will see to it that things are okay."

The girl remained silent. Jane put her hand on the girl's arm. But she pulled away, so softly that Jane did not notice until the black of her sleeve was no longer under her hand. "We will be gentle," Jane said to the boy, "but be careful of the others. They do not know Morocco and its women, they may not be so careful."

The boy smiled and said something to the girl in Moghrebi. Belquassim thought he heard, above the high-pitched voices of the room, "Keep away from her, she is mad and a drunk," and it saddened him. Jane would often drink too much, but he loved her nonetheless. And he knew she must have been thinking of their conversation about Moroccan women and why they wore the *haik*. Jane seemed so small tonight, her bravado was like the clothing she so admired in the *Vogue* magazine photographs. It just covered her body; underneath she was kind and generous, and she was being kind to the girl.

The film began. The voices quietened. Images of the school-girls, their grey uniforms dark against their white bodies, short skirts that came to the knee, legs opening for their punishment or their pleasure, eyes wide open, blonde German schoolmis-tresses, hair gold against the grey, long fingers, hands holding thin willow canes. The harsh guttural words that he could not understand flitted across the screen. He could not relate to the film, but because it was so different from what he was familiar with. It is actually quite exciting, he thought. He put his hand out and lifted Paul's hand from the table. For a long while he just sat there stroking Paul's hand and his bare arm. Paul did not respond, he seemed not to notice this touch, he was oblivious to everything except himself, but he did not remove his hand. Belquassim wondered if he could manufacture this feeling again. This quiet feeling of white skin under brown fingers, the sounds of Jane's breath close to his face. He wanted this to remain with him forever. Sounds of a film around him so that no-one could see into his private space.

The film was over. Voices all around talked about mesmeric teachers and boarding schools and uniforms and propaganda. Jane left the table to join a group of women who were sitting on the other side of the room. One of the women was dressed in a dress suit, she had a red necktie in the collar of her shirt and short black hair, she could have been a man. And another with her shivered in the cream silk dress that may have been her underwear. He could hear their laughter from where he sat. Paul drifted across the room to speak to his friend Bill who was playing cards with others in another corner of the room. Belquassim noticed how Bill's hands shook as they held the cards. They were playing bridge, and the stakes were high. But Bill and his partner would never win – how could they? Bill, who struggled so hard against whatever had captured him, was destined to lose. Or was he destined to lose? His self-created destruction could possibly make him more able to win than any other.

And so the evening wore on, weaving its loose pattern of morality over all who sat there.

At about midnight Paul and Belquassim left the café. Jane had already left with the woman in the dress suit. It was unlikely that she would be home before morning. Belquassim knew that Cherifa would come to the house to see if Jane was there, and when she could not find her she would go home, home to whoever waited for her. It was a short walk across the *medina* and up the hill to the *Petit Socco* where the house was. They walked side by side quietly, it was unnecessary to say anything – the lights on the hillside, the sound of the sea behind them and the smell of the city were sufficient.

They were walking down one of the myriad alleys in the *medina*. The sky was barely visible as the walls on the houses on either side of them seemed to arch over and meet each other in the middle. Suddenly from the large square a few metres to their left came screaming. A crack, and then there were more screams. "Hurry," said Belquassim taking Paul by the hand, "we must move away from here quickly, there will be violence, you know how it is."

Paul stopped, he took his hand out of Belquassim's, he was calm. He turned away from Belquassim and his voice was lapidary, "No, I want to hear these sounds. This is the sound of people who want to be free, free from the French who won't let them walk on their stinking bourgeois boulevards without being sneered at. And they think that if they are free of the French, if the Boulevard Pasteur is called the Avenue Mohammed V, they will be free from hunger and from nihilism. They won't you know, but it doesn't matter, what matters is their movement, their need to destroy those that they perceive are the cause of this wanton poverty and squalor. We are all its cause. We all want to destroy. I can't think of purity any more, it sickens me. I want to hear this."

The sounds seemed to get closer, Belquassim shrank into the wall of the small house – maybe it would cover him up and he would not be seen by either the Moroccan rebels or the French guards. But Paul started to move forward and he had to follow him, up towards the sound. There were more cries, they were closer now.

Belquassim heard the curses and the prayers, Arabic and Moghrebi. Then they were on the outskirts of the square. The moon was new, a mere slit in the sky, but the lights from the fires and torches of people brightened the whole area. A wild boy ran past them, a French guard following him. As quickly as the boy ran the Frenchman stopped and pointed his long handgun. The boy turned around and lifted his arms. Belquassim heard him cry out "Hamdoul'lah!" It was as if the boy understood that he would never say anything else ever again. Then there was a short sharp sound, and the image of the boy, his arms flung forward. The force of the shot propelled the rock from his hand, his body spun around, and Belquassim saw a small hole appear on his chest and then, as he spiralled, a gaping red stain starting to spread across his back. He swayed momentarily – it was as if he was diving into a distant pool – and then he slowly crumpled forward. The French guard, oblivious of his audience, put his gun into his belt and walked over to the boy. He spat on his face. A woman screamed. She ran up to the now silent boy. She knelt next to him keening, the sound was so slight and the breath so heavy. She pulled the boy up close to her breast and held him as a lover would, rocking backwards and forwards in time to the rattling of the background gunfire. The boy held on to her white robe. A bubble of blood slid like a jewel out of his mouth and she wiped it away with her sleeve, whispering. Then the coarse material of her dress fell languidly from his hand. She did not weep. The Frenchman moved forward and shot her in the back of the head.

Around them people continued to run, across the square, down the alleys, into the mosque. Paul and Belquassim stood and watched and listened, until, as quickly as the sounds began, so silence crept back into the square. Belquassim looked up. He could see the rose pink roof of the mosque outlined against the smoke and the sky, he saw the bicycles lined up against the walls of the shops and houses and he saw his reflection in the glass of the dead boy's eyes. He was crying now, but he did not know if he was crying for the boy, the woman or himself. The tears ran down his cheeks.

"It's like a photograph taken by Robert Capa," said Paul. His soul disappeared into the dark alley as he said these words. Belquassim turned and followed him from the square.

This was not the first or the last of the riots, as the French would call them, or the uprisings, as the Moroccans would say. But it was the first time that Belquassim had seen his reflection in the eyes of the dead.

XV

I am just a watcher. I have no sense at all that I can do anything that will change anything. I have no sense at all that even if I could change anything it would make any difference. I don't want to do anything. I don't want to make a difference. And anyway the universe is indifferent to us or our endeavours. How can we redeem ourselves? Through a community with other men as some have already put forward? Maybe we can even be lucid about this indifference. There is no prophylaxis, no solution. All I can do is write what I see and let other people be the judge of it. The comfort that there has to be a meaning in what I say and write just does not exist, that is mere sentiment, and a suspect conviction. I live in my own consciousness, as does everyone, but only I am able to acknowledge this.

Yesterday I was chatting to Bill. He derives his meaning from drugs, which is as meaningless as those that derive their meaning from killing other people. Nothing makes a difference. And while talking to him I remembered the days when I was a member of the Communist Party. In New York, of all places, I was a member of the Communist Party. And we all, including me then, thought that by being members we could change things. We thought that by blasting the system others would derive some goodness from it all. And then one day I just realised that it was all rubbish. Whatever happened in a room in New York, whatever we debated, the means of production and surplus value, whether or not what Stalin was doing could bring about socialism, none if it made any difference and none of it ever will. And no-one really cares.

I never want to go back to New York. I never want a place or a person to appropriate me. I will never take sides again, I do not have this right.

I never saw that boy who was killed, Paul and Belquassim just told me about it. The strange thing was that even as I heard Paul talking about it I felt that he was describing something that did not exist, it had not happened in reality. Something that was just a picture, a horrible picture, and yet he described it so beautifully. The words that he used were chosen so carefully, the woman who knelt next to the boy and who did not cry, the sound of the mosque calling people to prayer just at the moment of the boy's death, the small pinpoint of blood on the front of his shirt, but when he fell the hole in his back. It was as if he was writing something for one of his books, maybe he was just practising on me, seeing how I responded to the description. I obviously responded well, I felt a tear grow in each of my eyes and I brushed these tears aside. I tried to do this so that he would not notice, Paul always accuses me of sentimentality, but the tears just remained there. And Paul smiled when he saw this, he knew now that how he told the story could move a person. But there was no sentiment in his smile.

Belquassim told the story differently, he was afraid. Afraid I think to lose the city that he knows so well, and afraid that if foreigners are driven out we will go with them. And I think he was afraid that he might, one day, be that boy, a random arbitrary target in a war that was never made by him. A prophecy maybe. We all have to take sides sometime in our lives, and for Belquassim, he cannot really choose the side that he will ultimately be forced to take, despite Paul and me, and us. His side has already been chosen for him.

XVI

Belquassim and Paul walked across the square. The square where the killings had taken place. Belquassim looked at the stones that they walked on, he looked for a sign of anger, but there was nothing. It was midday and the sun aimed its rays at their foreheads. Paul wore a hat. When he put it on he laughed and said to Belquassim, "This really makes me feel like an outsider. My skin is too pale. The sun makes it change colour. I will never, no matter how hard I may try to, have that olive complexion that people who call this home have." He put the beige straw hat on his white hair and smiled. Touching the hat he said, "I have to create my own world here where I will not burn. If I do not create this world I will continue to burn until I can no longer think. And who wants to be bright red … and it is painful."

The square was busy. People moved everywhere. A woman selling apples and tomatoes, next to her a man who had old metal scraps on his blanket and next to him a herbalist who sold tonics for good health. On the north side of the square, next to a building that had pink walls and high windows, were thousands of bicycles. Belquassim wondered who rode them, although he knew that most people in the city owned one. He preferred to use a donkey or to walk. An old man wearing the traditional dress of a water seller walked close to them. On his back was a sack made of goatskin. It glistened as the water inside it moved out through the porous skin and into the air. He walked behind Paul and called out into him. A Nazarene, white, the colour of money. He called out "amen, amen". All Nazarenes were tourists, so all Nazarenes would buy his water so that they could wash their hands, wash their hands as they believed a Moroccan would wash his hands, not knowing that Moroccans did not do this any more, as there was a tap on every street corner. And then they would leave, they would return home, where they could no longer buy water from a man who was different to them. Paul walked on. He was a Nazarene, but he was a Nazarene who would not leave this city. This is his city, thought Belquassim, Paul has made it into his city, for here he can feel something different from hatred. He thought this now, but at other times he wondered if Paul did feel anything for this city. It was a place where Paul lived. It was the place where he had a roof to cover him. And it was the place where he could write. But it was just a city where he could be free.

They walked past a crowd of people. In front of a basket that held a snake stood a man. Belquassim bent his head and looked into the woven circle of grass. A dancing cobra. It lay motionless at the bottom of the basket, its hood thin and stretched. It was covered by gold leaf scales, which looked as if they had been especially crafted for this reptile. Snake jewellery, snake style, snake opulence, thought Belquassim as they walked. A sound pierced the sun. Paul stopped walking, he looked upwards from where the sound came. Above the basket in which the snake lay was a balcony. A man holding a wooded flute stood on it. He held the instrument to his thick purple lips. The skin of his cheeks moved in and out as he began to blow. Belquassim watched him as the notes edged their way downward. Slowly the man next to the basket began to move a thin silver rod above the body of the snake. It rose. At first the movement was slow, then the sounds of the flute became louder and faster, and the snake quickened its movements. Then it stood up. It flattened its head so that its gold leaf scales looked like a *haik*. Yet it showed people its eyes. The eyes of the snake were not covered by the glittering *haik*. They were black eyes, and in the harsh sunlight they appeared to be even blacker. The man moved the rod slowly. The snake followed the movement. The notes of the flute moved with the snake as it swayed. Around the basket a small crowd had gathered, Paul was the only Nazarene in the circle, watching. Four men stood up. At first they only knelt on their stone-grazed knees. Then they leaned back onto their haunches. Suddenly two of them jumped up. They let out a shout. And they began to dance. "It's the *Jilali*," said Belquassim. Paul and Belquassim watched them move. The dance was fast. There were no discernible steps to it. It was as if each of the men had something inside him, something that made the movements for him in the heat-filled air. Two of the other men then stood up and swayed. They swayed as the snake swayed. They followed the rod and the notes of the flute. A knife was passed by a woman in the circle to one of the men who was dancing. The blade was thin. He pulled it towards his chest and Belquassim gasped. He had seen this dance before, but every time he saw it he would think the same thing. He thought the man would insert the blade into his ribcage, up and into the soft flesh of his heart. He knew that the dancing man would not do this, but every time he saw the dance he imagined that this time he would do it, he would point the blade to his chest and pierce his heart. Instead he placed the blade on the inside of his naked thigh and pushed it downwards. The drop of blood flew through the air. And then another drop flew upwards, it flew through the sun. This one had come from the inside of his left arm. The knife moved, from the thigh to the arm, first the arm was sliced and then the thigh. A pool of red gathered on the ground. He smeared the blood on his face. The dance continued, jerky and uncoordinated. The same knife was now passed to the other man who danced. He too pressed it on his arms and his thighs. There was movement. There was frenzy.

There was music. And the green gold snake swayed. It did not miss a rhythm, even when the blood fell on its woven cage.

Belquassim stood with Paul and watched. "Come," said Belquassim, "you have seen this before, you know about the purifying dance. Come let's go. I do not like it. It makes me feel like a sinner. It makes me think that I am not pure."

Paul moved forward. "Yes," he replied, "you feel like a sinner." His tone was acquiescent, it was if he was agreeing with Belquassim, but Belquassim knew that Paul always acquiesced, even if he did not agree with what was said. "I do not feel afraid of sin," Paul continued. Now he spoke to himself.

A young man watched them as they moved away from the crowd. His eyes moved with them, out of the circle. The circle stood still as the men continued to dance. Belquassim heard a gasp, one of the men had fallen to the ground. Less than a minute later the other fell. Belquassim turned around and looked at them. The sweat from their bodies coagulated with the blood from their veins. Both bodies jerked a little as they lay on the dusty cobbles. The flute continued to play, the sounds were sweeter now. The green snake held its hooded mask up high.

Belquassim pulled at Paul. "Come," he said, "it is over." The young man who'd been watching the circle followed them. Paul and Belquassim walked across the square and followed the winding road down to the foreshore. Then they turned into the Café Hafa, where Paul was to meet Bill. Belquassim noticed that the young man had followed them from the square. His arms hung outside the shirt that he wore. He was muscular. He knew the streets. Bill was not yet in the café. Maybe he would not arrive – sometimes he did, sometimes not. Paul and Belquassim sat at one of the tables. The young man sat at another table, but close enough for them to see him if they chose to look.

"A coffee," Paul said to a waiter who approached the table. To Belquassim he turned and said, "It is the heat. I need the coffee in this heat, it makes me feel hotter. And I like to feel the heat. Not the heat of the sun of course." He laughed as he took off his hat and pulled his hand through his flattened white hair.

A small sound trickled into the café, two notes and then three. Belquassim looked up. The young man at the table had taken out what looked like a small *rhaita* from his bag. It was not as big as the traditional outdoor oboe-like metal instrument. He began to blow on it. His brown cheeks moved inwards as he drew in his breath and outwards as he blew. Paul looked up at him, holding the instrument close to his chest. "I must speak to him," Paul said. "See how he plays, listen to the sounds. Listen." Belquassim listened. The men in the café stopped talking as they too were held by the sounds. It was sweet, like unspoken words. It hung in the air between Paul and Belquassim.

"I must talk to this man who can make these sounds," Paul said. "When he is finished call him over here. Tell him that I want to talk to him."

"Why do you want me to call him?" asked Belquassim. For some reason he did not want Paul to speak to this man.

"You must ask him to come over here," said Paul. "He will not come to a Nazarene. He will think that I want to buy something, but I just want to talk to him."

Belquassim nodded. "Okay," he said. And to himself he whispered a thought: But he does have something to sell, and I do not want you to buy it. He saw us, he followed us, he wants you. But he got up from the table and walked over to where the *rhaita* played.

Belquassim greeted the man. He had dark hair and the look of the streets, a look that Belquassim knew he could have if he chose to. It was the look that Belquassim knew he would have had had he not met Paul. Paul had saved him from that look. Paul had given him the look of Tangier, the look of a biting hunger to know more, but in him the Tangier look was now tinged with the poetry of Europe. His face was like a coat with a blue silk lining. The outer layer of the coat had a Tangier beauty to it, and when Belquassim moved his hands across his eyes so that the inner part of the coat showed, only then could one see the lines of words under the outer material.

"*Salaam*," he greeted the man who played.

He moved the *rhaita* from his mouth and replied, "*Salaam*."

"The Nazarene, the man with the white hair, wants to meet you. He records music for the Americans," said Belquassim. "He wants to hear you play some more."

Belquassim knew that he had to put in the last part of his sentence. He knew, although it would make no difference, that he had to say that all Paul wanted was to hear the man play. He said it again: "The Nazarene wants to hear you play." It was said more for himself than for anyone else.

"Mohammed," said the man.

"Belquassim," said Belquassim.

The other looked at him. "I have seen the Nazarene before

today," he said. "I know that he wants the Moroccan music." Belquassim stared at him. His hands felt cold and dry even though the air in the café was hot and humid. Mohammed walked over to the table where Paul sat sipping his coffee. He walked in front of Belquassim. It was as if he already knew where he was going and what he was going there for. He sat down at the table. The *rhaita* was on his knee.

Belquassim sat at the table and listened while Mohammed spoke and Paul listened. It was as if he were not present. Mohammed was a storyteller. He made gestures, large and fierce, as he talked, he scowled and he exhorted. He presented a performance. Occasionally Belquassim would lift his hands and wave them above the table so that the flies would move off the coffee cups. But no-one noticed. This was his function, a fly sweeper. And Paul and Mohammed spoke about music. Mohammed spoke a lot. The streets and the music. Morocco and the music. His life and the music. Women and the music. He spoke as if he were telling a story. As Belquassim listened he was uncertain what was truth and what was not. But Paul listened anyway to this fantasy reality. Paul listened and did not interrupt. And Belquassim knew that all he wanted to do was listen to the voice, as once he had listened to the sound of Belquassim's voice. And Paul wanted to listen to the beautiful sound of the *rhaita*, for it was beautiful. Even Belquassim knew that it was beautiful.

There was a movement at the doorway to the café. A figure stood there. Tall and thin, the black felt hat at an angle. It was Bill. He swayed slightly as if he were in a dance, but it was not the purifying dance, it was the dance of a shaking hand and legs that would not come straight. He moved to the table. "Well, I am late," he said to Paul, "but who cares? There is no money in my time, nor yours."

"Sit," said Paul. "Have a coffee. Sit and listen to this." Paul turned to Mohammed and touched the *rhaita*, but he could have been touching Mohammed. It was a hot touch. Mohammed raised the instrument to his lips and played. Paul watched him. Bill lit a cigarette and watched its red tip.

XVII

When I listened to those sounds it was as if I did not exist. I know that I must record them, I know that even if no-one listens, I listen to the sound, but I must listen to it. Why do I need to keep the sound with me? I am not sure. When I listen to the notes I think that I am just a recording machine. A machine that will reproduce material that may exist after the machine is broken. And I will be broken one day. So the material that I record must continue to exist. That is the only justification for the existence of the machine in the first place, I suppose. I am a recording instrument rather than a person. I record music, the music of others and the music that I make. I record words, the words of others and the words that I make. So, whatever keeps the machine running, the food and the sleep that I need ... Well, I suppose I must take it for granted that it will go on.

And Mohammed is not only a music player. He tells a story. Maybe I should tell his story as well as play his music to the world. I can use the words of another. I can record the word sounds as well as musical sounds. Yes, I think that my next book will be a book that is the words of another. I like the confusion in Mohammed's stories. The confusion between reality and fantasy. For him they are all the same, the reality and the fantasy are a blur, so he lives in both of them. He is an actor, a man who lives in the myth. What he creates through his embroidery is spoken of as if it were true. He tells it as though it were true and I just listen, say, "Oh, really ..." I like the deviousness of his words. His talk of his suffering and the sounds of his music.

Strange how I listen to these stories of suffering. It makes me believe that the suffering of an American is a suffering that comes only from neurosis. But that, too, is real. It must be: Jane suffers.

I think the Nazarene will listen to me. I think the Nazarene will take me with him when he goes away from here. I think that I can go to America. I like the Nazarene. He listens when I talk.

XVIII

It was May, one of the hottest times of the year. Tangier seemed to be resting. Even the uprising seemed to lose its ardour in the heat. People and animals sat in the squares like orchids in a hothouse, occasionally moving their heads, to look up and drink in cool fresh water. Otherwise they sat, in the markets, in the cafés and in their houses, safe from the sun. It was not the best time of the year for guests to be arriving, but they were coming anyway. Gertrude and Alice, from Paris, and their friend, Natalie.

"Gertrude," Paul told Belquassim, "is large and formidable. She has a rich baritone voice and a laugh that emerges from the depth of her stomach. When I first met her she was already famous for poetry and plays. She has a way with words and sentences that is new and different. But she is also famous for her patronage of the new Parisian artists' movement. It was Gertrude who gave Picasso his first break. And Alice," he continued, "her companion, she has been Gertrude's lover for more years than I can remember, in fact, I do not know Gertrude without Alice."

"And who is Natalie?" Belquassim asked.

"Natalie," Paul replied, "is an American heiress. She has lived in Paris for a long while and owns a famous Parisian salon. The women of the Left Bank, and sometimes Picasso, gather there often, to drink and seduce each other. Natalie is coming with Gertrude and Alice as she wants to see Tangier and Jane – she has heard a lot about Jane from them – and so they agreed to take her on this trip."

Belquassim knew that it was Gertrude who had encouraged Paul to go to Morocco, and it was Gertrude who had told Paul to forget music and to write words. Paul had told Belquassim the story of how he had come to Tangier. "'Freddie,' Gertrude said to me when I was in Paris – she always calls me Freddie: my second name is Fredrick, and she said that Paul was a romantic name but I did not have an ounce of romance in me … So she said, 'Freddie, you must go to a place where you will be beyond life, where you can be an outsider, where you will be free of judgement and where you can write'. I would probably have gone anywhere then, but …" and he leaned over and kissed Belquassim, "I came here." He continued with a half smile on his face: "'You –' she said to me, 'If you do not work now when you are twenty, no-one will love you when you are thirty.' And now I am thirty, and who loves me, ha?"

But they were also taking this trip for another reason, a reason that was never discussed between Paul and Belquassim. Paul had met Mohammed, Mohammed, once a street boy like himself. Mohammed, wild and beautiful … Many times he had been in knife fights in the streets. He told his stories to Paul and played the traditional Moroccan music from the Rif Valley to accompany them. Paul was putting together a book of Mohammed's stories. Mohammed could not write, so Paul would sit with him for hours recording his words. Sometimes Mohammed would play on a *benedir*, a large flat disc-shaped drum, or on his *rhiata* and Paul recorded this sound too. Paul spent many hours with Mohammed, talking to him about his life and the stories that he wished to tell. A man who was not only beautiful, but who could tell a story. And in the hours that Paul and Mohammed spent together Belquassim could play no part. He would sit and watch them, heads lowered, the tape recorder whirring as Mohammed spoke and Paul listened and recorded. Belquassim listened to the sound of their voices and the short sharp laughter of Mohammed when Paul said something that he thought amusing or that he did not agree with. And he would watch, watch Mohammed's hand on Paul's thigh, watch their eyes as Mohammed stared, mesmerised by Paul.

Gertrude and Alice were a strange-looking couple, Belquassim thought when they arrived at the house in the *Petit*

Socco. Gertrude, stout and thickset, terse-mannered, but when she spoke her voice sounded as if it was emerging from a deep pool of water and her words were simple and beautiful. Alice followed Gertrude everywhere. She was tall but bird-like – she appeared to twitter, she was so bird-like. She sewed and cooked and kept their house in Paris. Belquassim could see that both of them loved Paul, Gertrude for his intellect and solipsism, Alice for his ability to create the images that she could not capture on her ever-present camera. And Jane? They seemed to treat her like an appendage of Paul's, always present but not quite a part of their circle of three. Belquassim had overheard a conversation between them on the day they arrived. They were standing in the bedroom, the room where Jane, when she was not with Cherifa, would sleep. Paul had asked Jane if she would give up her room for the period that Gertrude and Alice were in Tangier, and Jane had agreed. She had promised Paul that she would clear up the mess in the room. "This bedroom," Paul had said to her the day before Gertrude and Alice arrived, "looks as if Enola Gay has visited it. You must clear it up before Gertrude and Alice get here." His voice had an edge to it, as if he were speaking to an irresponsible child.

Jane, in her usual irritated way when she was angry, had replied, "I will." But by now she regretted her generosity in giving her room so freely to the guests. Belquassim had known that she would never clear it up.

"Really that woman is too much, both she and her book …" Belquassim heard Alice say to Gertrude, as he loitered outside on the staircase. "She fails to take responsibility for anything. She is like her characters, and it is Paul who has to bear the brunt of her idiosyncrasies. Why can't she for once behave like an adult? She is not a dependent child … She is after all out of her twenties …"

Gertrude, taciturn and non-judgemental, had not been so harsh – all she had said was, "It seems fine to me. Anyway, all we have to do is sleep here, and the sheets are clean." As he heard Alice speak, Belquassim thought that he understood why Jane had not cleared out the room. Why should she have? It was her life that Alice judged so harshly.

There was no room for Natalie in the small house and she was staying in a hotel closer to the beach. She said she preferred to stay where, as she said, "the action is". Soon Jane moved into the hotel with her. Before her arrival Paul had tried to warn Jane: "Don't fall in love with Natalie. She is a sybarite, she moves through women like a spirited stallion. No-one is ever around for very long." But, of course, this was only like giving Jane a chocolate and telling her not to eat it. She followed Natalie around with passion in her eyes, showed her the *souks* and even introduced her to Cherifa. Natalie was, of course, the spirited stallion Paul had described, but Jane seemed to enjoy the situation, until it ended.

Natalie would often come to the house, and Belquassim would watch her and Jane on the veranda at the top of the house. They would spend hours dressing up and swapping clothes, getting ready to go out. Jane loved the Parisian finery, the feminine silk Grecian dresses that Natalie had brought with her; and Natalie was fascinated by the boyish Moroccan trousers that Jane liked to wear. They would spend a long time in the house before setting out into the *medina*, staring at each other and themselves in the mirror. First Natalie would draw a line of black kohl under Jane's heavy-lidded deep-set eyes. Then she would take lipstick and spread the colour sensuously across her wide mouth. She would lean forward and kiss Jane, so that the red of Jane's lipstick met her own lips and they became stained with the kiss. She laughed as she draped a long glittering scarf over Jane's shoulders. With the scarf barely covering her breasts, Jane would walk across the room, as if she were a model for Coco Chanel, out on the catwalks of Paris. Coco Chanel, thought Belquassim, it sounds beautiful, it is a beautiful name. It is a name from Paris.

"Remember," Natalie told Jane, "you must always put your perfume where you think you will be kissed – the inside of your thighs, for instance." She laughed and picked up the crystal bottle, lifted the scarf and dabbed some of the incandescent liquid between Jane's thighs.

At other times they would lie together on a bed, or on the long tapestry-covered couch. Sometimes they made love, for Belquassim could only call those slow sensuous caresses love-making, he could not think of another word for it. Natalie would undo the buttons on Jane's shirt and move her long fingers, with their short blunt fingernails that were tipped in purple, over Jane's small upright breasts. Her fingers would move for a long time, they never seemed to be in a hurry, slowly grasping, twisting and stroking the dark nipples. And Jane would arch her back, moving in towards Natalie's hands, wanting more of her touch. At other times, it was not lovemaking, not the slow gentle movement of fingers on the tips of a breast or between pulsating legs. At other times they seemed almost violent in the way they sought out each other's bodies. Jane, on her knees in front of Natalie, moving her mouth along and up Natalie's thighs, under her long Paris dress, moving upwards, touching and reaching inside. And Natalie would cry out as the tip of a tongue met that wet space that gives so much pleasure. And when she twisted the skin on Jane's arm in a hard brutal way Jane would gasp as if she were a frangipani bud that had been torn from the branch.

They seemed to share a slow sensual light-heartedness, Jane and Natalie. But sometimes, when the fantasy world of Natalie was over for the day, Jane would come into Paul's room at night. Belquassim watched her curl up like a small animal, some primal thing, in Paul's arms. They would lie on the bed, Paul would stroke her shoulders and back and whisper into her hair. Sometimes he would read to her, sometimes he would just hold her gently and silently. At times he would get up off the bed and close the door, and the murmuring sounds would mingle with the dark air. Belquassim knew not to disturb Paul and Jane at moments like this, this was their private love, one that no-one could interfere with.

With Natalie in Tangier, Jane had no time for Cherifa. She seemed to forget the obsessive love that she shared with the market woman. Cherifa watched with her elongated black eyes, and waited. She knew that her time was not over. Natalie would tire of her plaything and return to her exotic life in Paris. Belquassim knew this too.

They planned a journey through the country. Paul suggested going to the Sahara. Gertrude refused, saying that despite the fact that she loved the heat, the Sahara would be just too much. Also, as in Tangier, the uneasy restlessness of people was everywhere in the desert towns bordering Algeria. In any event, she and Alice wanted to see the more traditional side of Morocco – Fes, Meknes, and the Roman ruins at Volubis. Jane did not seem to care where they went as long as she was with Natalie. Eventually it was decided that they would take two cars, Paul hired a large black Mercedes Benz that pre-dated the war. Gertrude, who loved to drive – she had learnt to do so during the war when she and Alice would carry sick and wounded soldiers to hospitals in the ravaged French countryside – would drive it. Paul would drive his own car.

The convoy stopped many times along the way for Alice to take photographs, so it took the best part of a day to get to Fes. Natalie and Jane, during these short interludes of the journey, would lie in the back of the car, whispering, kissing each other – silent long kisses.

Jane was trying to write again. On the journey she wrote pieces for the characters in her book. On one of these stops Jane called to Belquassim, "Come, listen to my paragraph, tell me what you think of it." She told him, "Once I wrote about Mrs Perry. She lives alone. She is a dreamer who wants only plain pleasures, plain pleasures, without crowds and fancy food. Maybe this new character is too much like Mrs Perry. I don't know. I must ask Paul what he thinks of this new work. I am writing now, but am I writing exactly what I have written before?" Belquassim leaned into the window of the big black car listening. Natalie just smiled.

"*I remember when the pigeon coop was in the garden.*" Jane read from her notebook. "*After the rains the wood smelled damp and unsafe, the white pigeons mingled insatiably with each other, never enough. Now there are no more birds. Only the wooden beams remain. There has been no rain; the birdhouse is still and in shadow.*

I remember the odour of the birds, bitter almonds, somehow enticing. I remember when you built the pigeon coop outside in the garden. It smells damp and unsafe." She scratched out a word and replaced it with another. "I'm not sure that I am getting it right ... Well, what do you think?" Natalie said, "Umm umm," and smiled.

Belquassim leaning in the window somehow felt that Jane was writing for both of them, the danger of their loves and hopes. All he could say however was, "It's lovely, and sad, and maybe it reminds me too much."

Then Paul called to him and he got back into the car and they resumed their journey. Soon Belquassim could see the white buildings of Fes in the distance. It was different from other Moroccan cities, being mostly white – new white stark buildings built by the Arabs. Only the *medina* had the pinkish tinge of familiarity.

There were seven gates to the old city. The small party entered by one that was not much used. A very small donkey carrying a huge load of goods blocked their path, and they had to wait for it to move on and into the winding alleys. The man behind it shouted in Moghrebi, "*aserdon, aserdon*" and beat it with a thin switch. The donkey could hardly move because of the load. It is a donkey's destiny to carry the burdens of man, the burdens of a master, thought Belquassim. Paul took the party to a small hotel just inside the city gate, and then he and Belquassim left the others to find Mohammed. Mohammed seemed to be everywhere in Paul's life now. Paul did not seem to care whether Belquassim accompanied him when he saw Mohammed, so Belquassim accompanied him anyway. He would think to himself, it is because Paul is still unfamiliar with the Moghrebi language. Or he would think, maybe, just maybe Paul wants me to go with him. He needs me to help him if he should not understand what the words really mean, or how to write them down exactly.

Paul's idea was to write down these stories and also to make a tape recording of Mohammed's music. "In this way," he said to Belquassim, "I am giving something back to this country, this place that gives me the space to create. My name will ensure that Mohammed's work, real Moroccan work, is published and read by the rest of the world. And the music, I know, will be strange for people in New York, but I think they will find that it will linger with them long after they have heard it, so they will want to buy it and keep it. Keep it for themselves."

On one of the evenings Mohammed arranged for Jane and Alice to have their hands painted with henna by his sister. Jane loved decorations. She told Paul, "To decorate the body is like giving it a gift. I like putting clothes on my skin. It protects me." Mohammed came to fetch them from their hotel early in the evening. Paul was already at the house. Gertrude remained at the hotel, writing. Natalie was out, seeing the city.

The doorway to the house was low. Alice, who was tall, stooped to enter. Over the entrance was a silver Hand of Fatima, placed there to keep the house safe. Mohammed's family lived in two small rooms, on the second floor of the narrow building. They walked up the narrow stairs in single file. From the outside the building was just like any other. Inside, it buzzed with decoration. A picture of the tomb of Moulay Idriss, in the sacred town just outside Meknes, was pinned on the wall above the stove. Next to it was a calendar with pictures of European cities. The picture for May was of London Bridge, spread-eagled across the Thames. All around, the room was cluttered with furniture, a chair, a large bed, and several tables. All were covered with the brightly coloured fabric that was found in the *souk*. Jane sat down in a chair next to the stove. It was hot in the small room. Mohammed's sister, Lydia, was preparing henna, which she would use to paint their hands. For a long time she strained the greenish leaves, pushing them through small holes in a sieve. Belquassim, who had seen his mother do this many times tried to explain to Jane and Alice why it was taking so long. "The henna has to be fine," he said, "like powder before it gets mixed with water, otherwise it will not sink into the skin. And the lines must not be too thick because this makes them uneven and then the pattern is indistinct." Lydia strained the leaves over and over again. She then took the fine powder and mixed it with water so that it became a paste, and filled a small syringe with the mixture.

Jane put out her right hand, having chosen a simple geometric design for her hands, Alice chose something more elaborate. Lydia took one of Jane's hand's in her own brown one. Jane's hand shook a little and the fine blue veins stood out on her wrists. Lydia steadied the hand gently. The picture grew on Jane's hand, crept up her arm and moved over her fingers. The picture was green and then, slowly, it took on the muddy red colour that was so familiar to Belquassim. He tried to remember his mother's hands stroking his head: he saw the design on her arm, a picture that had been drawn right up to her elbows, and he remembered looking down at her hard cracked feet which were also decorated, covered in flowers. He could not see her face.

And then it was Alice's turn. "Don't touch anything," Lydia said to Jane. "If you do the henna will rub off, and then you would have come here for nothing."

While Alice had her hands painted, Jane danced around the room swinging her arms, "I am trying to get it to dry quickly," she said. "I need my hands tonight."

After the painting was over Lydia made them coffee. They sat in the hot room drinking it. Behind a thin curtain Belquassim could hear the murmured voice of Mohammed with the occasional interjection from Paul. They waited for Mohammed to complete his story before leaving.

"I feel sick," said Paul. "It must be something that I ate, I am not used to eating so much from the street. Or maybe it's that amoebic dysentery that I caught when I was in Mexico. They say it never goes away." It was early evening and they were sitting in a restaurant in Meknes. Belquassim felt tired, as well as worried about Paul. Paul did not often feel sick, but today his face was white and drawn.

Alice was telling him about Moulay Idriss. He already knew the story – Belquassim had told it to Paul himself. But Paul listened to Alice anyway. "It is one of the holiest sites after Mecca. Thousands of Muslim pilgrims go there each year. If they can't get to Mecca they go to Moulay Idriss. He was the founder of the first Islamic kingdom in Africa, you know. It's such a pity that we could not go inside, I would have loved to see the floor mosaics – apparently they are spectacular. I sent Belquassim in to try and take a photograph, but ..." she looked at Belquassim "... well, he said he would not take the picture – he would just look at the floor and then describe it to me. Has he told you that taking a photograph is like taking a part of the soul, for people and for buildings? Strange. So I didn't get my picture but I got a description. Oh and then Jane ..." She turned to Jane as she spoke. "You do describe things so well – doesn't she Gertrude? – Jane wrote it down for me." Natalie yawned, she had heard Alice on similar subjects before. Jane tucked her hand into Natalie's arm, and Gertrude, who never said anything unless it was necessary to speak, said nothing, just carried on eating and putting sentences together in her head as if no-one else was at the table. Alice continued: "Do you know how I travel, Paul? I am sure Gertrude has told you about this. I find a book written by a traveller. I first read it at home, and then plan my trip along the same route. And then I read it again while I am travelling. In this way I get two experiences, mine and the other person's – it's like going away twice."

"I don't think that you are a traveller," said Paul suddenly and harshly, "I don't think any of you are travellers," he said, sweeping the table with his eyes that were cold and blue. "You are all tourists. And why ...?" he continued. "It's about time. The tourist rushes home after a few weeks or even months. The tourist has a home to return to. A traveller belongs to nowhere specific so he moves slowly from one part of the earth to another, never belonging, never settling. Like Port, in my novel." His eyes for an instant had a look of bitterness in them, and then he lowered his head.

The tomb of Moulay Idriss, thought Belquassim during the conversation, is more than just holy. It's our history, a history that cannot be tainted by anyone else. He thought about the green mosaics that covered the roof of the mausoleum, the arch of the dome reaching high above his head, dwarfing everything around it. He thought he could hear the sound of the *muezzin* calling from the roof of the mosque, but the call was only in his head as the mosque was far away. The call seemed to spread out across the green fields that occupied the space behind them. I am glad she was not allowed inside, he thought. It is a space only for us Moroccans, a space that is holy, a space that cannot be ruined. Around them in the café the hum of Moghrebi could be heard. The company was mostly men, few women ate outside their homes. But their group sat apart from the Arabs. He was not a part of them now. It's true, thought Belquassim, I am moving, as a traveller does, through a world that we can only look at. I feel lost from everything. And for a second, a short transitory second, he wondered if it was all worthwhile.

Outside the café sat a woman. She was perched, a bit like a bird with her long Semitic nose, on a high chair, and the chair had been placed inside a box-like structure. Her head was covered with an embroidered scarf, her eyes shining through the narrow gap in the material. She was selling unleavened bread. Alice took out her camera and focused on the woman. "She is beautiful," Alice said. "It's such a perfect shot." Suddenly the woman, who had at first seemed so impassive, started to shout angrily. She waved her arms in the air in violent gestures. Above the noises of the street Belquassim heard her telling Alice to take her camera elsewhere, but Alice of course could not understand.

"I told you," Belquassim said to Alice. For the first time he felt real anger. "You can't take photographs of people. Photographs take away a person's soul. You must ask them first, and even then it is unlikely that they will allow you to. You can't take away their souls." Alice was fumbling in her bag. "It's not money she wants. Just put away your camera. We are not all for sale here." He felt that she was an intruder, taking something she neither understood, nor wanted to understand, taking it purely for her own sense of possession.

A small crowd gathered around them. Jane and Natalie disappeared around a corner. Paul and Belquassim spoke to the man at the front of the crowd. He had a stick in his hand and his face was more red than brown. "Go home, Nazarenes, go home!" he repeated over and over again. "The Prophet does not want you here." It took a while, and all Belquassim's powers of persuasion, to make him believe that Alice was just a foreigner and that not all Nazarenes were the same. Paul, after all, spoke Moghrebi. The crowd slowly dispersed.

Alice was shaking, Gertrude looked furious, her eyes blazing, then walked away from them and into a small shop that sold postcards and other artefacts for tourists. Belquassim saw her turning the steel stand that held a number of postcards. She picked one and went to the counter to pay for it. A minute later she emerged from the shop. She handed the postcard to Alice. "Your photograph," she said. On the card was a picture of a woman seated on a high chair placed inside a box-like structure. Her nose was long and Semitic. On her head was an embroidered scarf. She was selling flat unleavened bread. She no longer had a soul, it had already been taken from her.

And on they moved, to Volubis, an old Roman town. It was more than two thousand years old and deserted. The grey stone of the ruined buildings loomed over their heads as they walked through the old town. Paul was not with them, he had chosen to stay at the hotel in Meknes. Alice was reading to them from a book, while Gertrude said nothing – she did not need to speak to engulf a person. Jane and Natalie were leaning over one of the low stone walls and gazing into the distance. Natalie then took out her camera. "Click, click, click." She took many photographs, Jane sitting pensively on the low wall, her head turned sideways, then looking ahead, sometimes just staring into the distance, other times her head seeming to spin on her shoulders, always with that strange lost look in her eyes. She seemed to be looking for something, but here, with the ghosts of the Roman slaves hovering around them, she did not seem to be able to find what she was looking for. The camera winder whirred in the air … Jane, Jane and Jane. Belquassim wondered if he would ever see these pictures. I would like to, he thought, so I can remember this journey, Jane next to the one-dimensional people riding horses and carrying baskets who are on the mosaic floors of some of the buildings, a mosaic memory.

Belquassim walked towards the massive gate that stood at the entrance of the old city. Standing behind it he could see the rolling green hills through its arch, moving as if with their own momentum. Jane came up and stood behind him. She took out an apple from her bag and gave it to him. "Some sweetness," she whispered, and wound her arms around him. Then she ran off and he was left alone again, wondering about love and the feel of her arms around him and hoping that it would last as long as the ruined city.

"Well, it sounds like your day was good," muttered Paul, when they met later at a coffee bar. "Better than mine ... This godforsaken nausea, I hate feeling ill. I hate feeling that I can't control my body." He turned to Jane, and said, "Remember that time in Mexico, when I was so sick I could not move for a week, and I was always vomiting, I think that the same bacterium has reared its head again. It is swimming through my intestines, or maybe it has had children and now they are swimming." He shivered.

Jane smiled at him and stroked his hair, moving her hand gently across his wet forehead. "Let's go back to the hotel," she said to him. They got up, she steadying him and he leaning heavily on her thin shoulders.

Belquassim stood up too. "No stay," said Paul, "I want to be alone tonight." Alone, thought Belquassim, alone means alone with Jane. He felt a shiver run down his body. A feeling of exclusion engulfed him, swallowed him up, but he sat down nonetheless. Jane and Paul walked out of the coffee bar and to the car. He heard the sound of the motor as it started up, rasping harshly through the thicket of sounds that pervaded the inside space.

Natalie continued to stare at the pictures on the wall of the café. Gertrude started a conversation with Alice about a cookbook she was writing. "It's unique," Alice said. "I am going to have people's recipes in it – lots for you, one for Picasso, and some for Paul and Jane." She stood up. "And," she continued, "it's going to have photographs in it, like this one." Her camera clicked, Belquassim leaned forward to rearrange the cups and sweetmeats on the table. "No!" he heard her exclaim, "I don't want your hand in the picture, it must be pristine, just the dishes." He moved his hand out from the frame. And the camera clicked once again.

And then the journey was done, and they went back to Tangier. Jane, Natalie, Gertrude, Alice, Belquassim and Paul had completed their journey.

XIX

Gertrude is a woman who makes me want to love her. She is not beautiful. In fact she is ugly. She is short and fat. Her hair is cropped and she wears those strange shapeless dresses. But I love her voice. I love its sound. I love her space. She makes me want to drown inside her.

And Natalie, she makes me want to prove myself. I am not stupid. I am not plain. And yet with Natalie I feel insecure. I feel plain and I feel stupid. I am not part of the world that she comes from. And so she can do whatever she wants with me. And I laugh as if everything that she wants I want too. And now she is gone, so I no longer have to prove myself. Now I can be alone in my city. Now I can feel secure again. But Gertrude is not here either ...

❧

Gertrude told me to write. Gertrude introduced me to words. Gertrude is someone who is so like me ... Or maybe I am so like her. Maybe it is I that tried to make myself like her.

I hate being a tourist.

It is a new thing for me to record the story of another. Yes, I do make some changes, but the story and the language are not my own. Now I am playing with the words of another. They are not my words. I do not own them. Yet I feel that they are mine because I write them down.

I like my fiction because writing fiction means I know that I am impermanent. There are no victims, for all the victims are made out of words. And so I leave no victims in this world. Now that I am thinking of permanence, I wonder if there is permanence. If anyone does leave a trace behind, then this trace must be erased. It must be removed. People must not be visible when they are not there. They can only be visible when they are in the space. When they are gone, any trace − a cigarette, a work of fiction, a poem – must be removed, erased.

And yet I write fiction. And when I die my books will remain, and if they are still read people will remember me. Or maybe they will not. Maybe they will just remember the people who are made by the words. They will not be my words. They will just be words. People's words.

Feeling sick makes me think about death. Feeling something in my stomach makes me think that when I die I will not be able to feel the worms or whatever it is that come to crawl on my body. I will never know what will live on my skin. Nothing lasts, but does it pass on?

XX

"I can't do it, I can't do it any more! Why are you forcing me? You know that I can't do it." Jane's rage filled the house.

"I'm not forcing you," Paul said, speaking slowly and with infinite care, "I'm just trying to encourage you to use your talent, and it's a real talent no matter how you denigrate it."

Jane picked up the glass that was on the table next to her and threw it up against the low ceiling. The glass shattered, the liquid dripped downwards to the floor, opaque in the dim light. "You make me feel so impotent. Day after day you sit there and I hear the sounds of your fingers on the keyboard of that dilapidated typewriter of yours. And then what happens? You publish a book that people love. And what do I do? I sit and listen to your fingers while mine stay immobile." She turned and said bitterly, "You weren't supposed to be a writer, I am the writer. You made music, beautiful music. We complemented each other. Why did you have to write? I hate you for being a writer. I hate you for making me feel like this."

Paul sat still, impassive, a drop of liquid, then another, fell onto his outstretched hand resting on the arm of the chair. In his other hand was a letter he had just received and had been reading to Jane and Belquassim. A letter from New York, a letter with a newspaper cutting attached to it. The thick black words that made up the headline seemed to sever the small piece of paper in half, "*Sexual perversion, spiritual bankruptcy, violence, madness, nihilism – a novel touched with genius*" it read. The words blurred in front of Belquassim's eyes. He looked at Paul, who said nothing, just looked at Jane. Sorrow spread across his mouth. Then, as suddenly as Jane's anger had erupted, so it drifted away. She walked out of the room and down the passage into the kitchen. A shadow remained in the silence. Belquassim reached out to touch Paul, but he pushed him away.

When Jane returned she held a broom and a cloth. She bent and wiped the drops from Paul's hand. She took the letter and the newspaper cutting from him and tried to dry them. When there was no moisture left she handed them back to Paul. Then she used the cloth to dry the floor; the liquid from the glass had stained the wood. Belquassim picked up the broom. "No," Jane said, "don't." The shattered glass sparkled in a small pile, it clung to the straw fibres of the broom and twinkled in the dull glow of the lamp. She stopped the restless sweeping and turned to Paul. "I'm sorry, I'm so sorry. It's not you that I hate, it's … I don't know what it is …" she said. She crouched down. The broom fell from her hands as she knelt at Paul's feet rocking, holding him around his knees. "Forgive me … It's just … I can't produce anything that makes you think that I am worth anything. I can't fight this war any more. I can't do it any more."

Paul crumpled the letter and the cutting and threw it onto the floor. "Neither can I," he said, and pushing her aside he left the room.

Jane sat next to the window, the broom at her feet, the crumpled letter with the newspaper cutting attached to it moving lightly in the breeze. She leaned over to pick it up. She looked at the written words of the letter and read them out loud. "'*Dear Paul,*'" she read, "'*Enclosed is a review of your book, it is one of many that have been published in the New York press, all of which are equally flattering. This cutting is the review published in* The New York Times *on 10 June. As you can see, you are now a celebrity. You are not only loved by the small circle that surrounds you, but by the world at large. For myself I never had any doubts that this would be the case, once you put your mind to it. There is now no doubt in the eyes of the American public that you left behind, no doubt at all, that you are one of the finest writers of modern fiction. Your work will stand alone in the history of contemporary literature. Why don't you come over to NYC this fall? Although the book needs no further promotion, it would be great for you to see how it has been acknowledged by the literary set. Wystan particularly wants to congratulate you. All my love, T.*

P.S. Send love to Jane, and tell her to persevere with her work. There is still some support for her play on Broadway."'

Jane put the now stained letter onto her knee and tried to fold it along its original lines, but somehow she could not seem to iron out the creases. Then she got up from her chair, walked slowly across the room and pinned the cutting from *The New York Times* to the small noticeboard that hung on the wall above the long wooden table where they would sometimes sit and eat at night. She pinned the piece of newspaper next to a photograph of Paul and herself on the beach at Rabat. In Paul's hands was a book – the book that Jane had written. Belquassim could see the title on the front of it: *Two Serious Ladies*. She then went into the kitchen and poured herself a drink. The whisky was dark, with no water mixed into it. It rolled viscously against the smooth sides of the glass as she sat down again. The window was open and the breeze blew in the dust and smells from the harbour. The dust settled over Jane's small frame and coated her so that the colour of her blouse was dulled by the colour of the air. The smells of raw fish and frankincense invaded the space, and engulfed the small house. But the odours did not bring gifts, only an evil dark smell.

Belquassim sat and watched her. She quietly turned to him and said, "The book was about us, you know. Oh, I know Paul will say that he only used some aspects of our relationship as the model for the marriage in the book, and that was all. But I know that the relationship is ours. I am that woman, I am Kit and Kit is me. And he is Port, and Port dies in the end. Paul lives out the death of Port, he lives out that dying. I don't care if I go mad like Kit, but I don't want Port to die. And he dies after Kit has abandoned him. Have I abandoned Paul? Have I abandoned him with my jealousy? Have I betrayed him because I feel he has usurped me as the writer?" She looked down at her glass, then she raised her head and, as if she wanted Belquassim to hear her, she said, "In our world, is there a distinction between the one who does the betraying and the one who is betrayed, between the one who does the abandoning and the one who is abandoned? I am so afraid, so afraid that it is a prophecy, and that what we have is slipping away. It's too precious to let slip away. And I can do nothing about it, I can't even write any more." She held her head in her hands. "Paul needs only himself to be able to do what he does – least of all, he needs me. And because he does not need me, I want to hurt him. My picayune attempts at writing, and my neediness detracts from his successfulness and drains him of his energy."

She turned once again to the window, and Belquassim saw her face reflected in the windowpane. He could see in her reflection the deadness of her eyes as they stared out into the distance. But he could not see the Jane he knew any more. He saw only a reflection, a woman who, despite the fact that Paul had not said so, had harmed him, an immeasurable harm. And Belquassim hated her for that, he could never forgive her for creating the space for Paul to move further away and into himself, thus increasing the distance between Paul and himself. He saw three tears run down her cheeks – pearls of water like the pearls of her necklace that had touched his face on the day that they had first met – and then more of them spreading from her eyes and mingling with the black of her make-up. Belquassim felt his face close, his mouth twisting in a bitter hatred for her. He knew that he could never elicit from Paul a response that was as powerful as Jane had provoked. She had the capacity to harm Paul as he never could, and for this he could not forgive her. Her eyes closed momentarily as if to block out his hatred, but when she opened them again and looked at him, she could see that the depth of his dark eyes held neither warmth nor comfort. Belquassim loved only a memory now, a memory of how her love had created him, a memory of her love for Paul. He got up and moved towards her, his fists clenched tightly together. It was as if he meant to hit her. Then his fingers unfurled and he put his hand on her shivering shoulders. He felt the bones under his fingers as they tightened.

"Don't touch me!" She spoke harshly. "I don't need your pretence at affection." But she was not speaking to him – it was Paul that she addressed. He leaned down and, like a traitor, laid a silver kiss on the top of her head.

Paul was sitting in the room that he called his study. A record that he had given Jane for her last birthday played in the background, American blues. The trumpet filled the small space. Belquassim knew that Paul hated what he termed "new American music without lyrics, without tone and without originality", but he was playing it now. The sound of Miles Davis rose in the air of the hot room. It coated Paul, his hair shone under harsh silver light. The lamp made a golden pool on the desk, its circular shape making shadows of the typewriter and papers that Paul was staring at. He was looking at the manuscript of Mohammed's book: in his own handwriting were Mohammed's stories of pain, Mohammed, who was now a part of his life, yet a side of life that Paul could only observe. Next to him lay a page, on which was a poem, one that reflected the only kind of pain that he did know but would never acknowledge. At the top of the page were the words *"To Jane"*. Paul picked up the poem and, looking at Belquassim, he began to read it aloud, or rather he was reciting it from memory:

At first there was mud, and the sound of breathing,
and no-one was sure where we were.
When we found out, it was much too late.
Now nothing can happen save as it has to happen.
And then I was alone, and it did not matter,
Only because by that time nothing could matter ...
We thought there were other ways.
The darkness would stay outside.
We are not it, we said. It is not in us ...
There was a time when life went along brighter lines.
We still drank the water from the lake,
and the bucket came up cold
and sweet with the smell of deep water.

Paul stopped speaking for a moment. He opened the desk drawer and took out some tobacco and hashish. He rolled a hash stick leisurely, as if he felt relaxed, but his hands shook as he crushed the thick, sticky, black paste into the tobacco. He rolled the hashish and tobacco into the paper that he held between his thumb and forefinger, bent down and licked the sides of the paper. It cut a small line on his tongue and the blood made a pink stain on the thin white cigarette. He lit the hash stick and drew on it. The smoke rose with the heat to the ceiling, making cloud-like patterns in the arc of the desk light. The music continued to play. Paul continued to speak:

> The song was everywhere that year, an absurd refrain:
> It's only that it seems so long, and isn't.
> It's only that it seems so many years,
> and perhaps it's one.
> When the trees were there I cared that they were there,
> and now they are gone.
> On our way out we used the path that goes around the swamp.
> When we started back the tide had risen.
> There was another way, but it was far above and hard to get to.
> So we waited here, and everything is still the same.
> There were many things I wanted to say to you
> before you left, and now I shall never say them.
> Though the light spills onto the balcony
> making the same shadows in the same places,
> only I can see it, only I can hear the wind
> and it is much too loud.
> The world seethes with words. Forgive me ...

When he had finished Paul said, "And now I must put this away, my allegiances are after all to myself." He opened a yellow cardboard file and put the poem inside it. Then he added to Belquassim, "Come and sit here. Take off your shirt, I want to look at you and I want to touch you." The darkness was sinister, and the light from the lamp made the room glow like an undeveloped film. Belquassim took off his white shirt. It was wet with sweat and clung to his arms as he pulled it over his head. His body was stiff. Paul leaned over and took a nipple between his fingers, on which the black residue of the hash stuck to his skin. He held the nipple without a caress. Then he brought the lighted hashish stick close to the small raised nipple, until Belquassim felt it hot against his skin. He tried to move away but Paul held him close. "Do you think I am going to burn you?" And he laughed at Belquassim's fear. A drop of salty sweat ran down Belquassim's chest, and the liquid sizzled in the bright fire of the hash cigarette.

"What is cruelty?" Paul asked. "How does it manifest itself in these types of love? Is it the cruelty of arbitrariness, or the cruelty of insecurity, or the cruelty of a deliberate exercise of some indiscernible power? I am discovering secrets about love which I never knew of before ... But," he continued – it was almost as if he were talking to a mirror, not to Belquassim at all, "I want to make a case for love. You may not think that I have the right to, but I will anyway. I believe that if you are in love there is never any guarantee that you will ever be loved back."

"Turn around," Paul said. He said it quietly, it was not a command, but rather a yearning plea, a yearning for closeness and flesh. Paul moved his free hand down Belquassim's naked skin, softly touching the thin column of bones that filleted his back; he brought his other hand to his mouth and took another long drag on the hashish. His hands moved gently. For a moment the caress stopped, and where the warm fingers had been it was cold. Belquassim heard Paul taking off his clothes. Miles Davis filled the space in his head with notes that were menacing. The voice seemed inhuman. Maybe it was the record on the turntable. "Love is only valuable if it is instinctive, rather than rational," Paul went on. "I don't need to be loved back by anyone. I love her more than I have loved anyone. But my love is selfless, because, in a sense, if I am in love with my own reflection, it's a reflection that I see in her. And in this I stand alone. It's possible then that I am the cruel one." There was a perfect balance between gentleness and violence in the voice. It was then that Belquassim felt the fire of the hashish burn into his shoulder. His shoulder blades convulsed. He looked down and saw the skin bubbling up like animal fat in a pan when a woman is cooking meat. Paul pushed the lighted coal harder into him. With the pain of the burn he felt Paul thrust inside him. Instinctively he tried to pull away, but he could not move. Their sweat mingled, and the pain shrugged its way across his shoulder, then it was gone. In his body was a strange and particular delight.

For a long time afterwards they lay next to each other on the floor of the study. Paul licked his fingers and put them to the raw burn on the smooth brown flesh. "It's nothing," he said, "only another scar." Belquassim only murmured into Paul's hair, sweet quiet words, recapturing moments of rationality, moments of another time. Butter, he thought, I must find some butter to put on the burn.

XXI

Maybe I must be content with never sleeping close to someone, never really being held in someone's arms. Does that sound needy? Maybe it does, but I don't really care any more. I know that I sleep in the arms of so many women, but it's not the same. Or is it the same? These questions, such a cliché, the questions that everyone asks once in a while. Maybe I must just value what I have with Paul, but even that I have lost. I have done terrible and irreparable damage.

I can be cruel when I feel that I am in danger, and I was so cruel. And it is such irrational cruelty because it does not change anything, it just destroys. I feel abandoned by Paul, in both a physical sense in that we seldom touch each other any more, and because in his mind he has already moved away from me into that world of nothingness where he is able to create. He needs to watch someone die, implacable and without feeling, and then he writes about it, and he writes about it beautifully. I know he wrote about the death of that boy: he had his pencil in his mouth after the night of the killings and he was thinking how to write it down. And now he is gone, moved away from me. And then my anger, it's anger because I feel abandoned, but it is also anger, irrational and immature anger, that his books are doing so well. I am the writer, I write with feeling, I put everything that I have done or felt or thought into my stories, and I can no longer do it. Maybe because I have no feeling left without him.

And his books, which he writes without feeling, his books about the meaning of nothingness, those are the ones that do well. And this therefore is a second betrayal – I have lost him, and his success is a rejection of all that I believe in. And because I feel betrayed, not only once but also twice, I push and push and push him, to measure his response. It is like a test to see if he loves me. If he loves me he will continue to do so despite my cruelty, it is a test that I put everyone *through. To pass the test is not to abandon me, to fail is to leave. And he is leaving, he has left already.*

No-one has ever passed the test.

Yet I know that Paul will never find anyone who could love him more than I do. It's a strange sort of love, but it is more love than he will ever see in his whole life. And as I feel my tears start up in my eyes I wonder if he will remember this love, or if, now that he is gone, he will only remember my cruelty.

I wonder why Paul has not hit me. I deserve this violence. He hit me once before, why does he not do it now.

❧

I have to get out of here. I have to get away from this claustrophobic city where every expatriate knows every other expatriate, but where no-one knows the real people of this city. I must get out because otherwise I cannot write, and because I cannot write I will go mad.

I have made plans to travel to the island. There at least the air is clean, there are none of the fumes of searches with no ending, the wretched smell of nothingness does not permeate the air there. At least there I can write about this absurdity they call the world, this sentimental quest for meaning that everyone seems to embrace. "Do you believe in love?" someone asked me the other day, and I replied, "Love, I don't care enough about anything so how can I know if I believe in it? And it is an absurd abstraction, love. What is it anyway?" I love myself. I am condemned I suppose to a life-long sentence of solitary confinement within the closed-in space of my own consciousness.

And where is Jane in all of this? Do I care about her or is she just my wife? I have lost what little sentimentality I had, and it is time to move on, move on into my own self-created solitary confinement. I must move on so that I can at least live and eat and breathe without having every day to be reminded that there are those who still think that there is a world of reason, a world of feeling, a world in which human beings can discern meaning. I must move on so that I do not become crippled by others pressing down on me, paralysing me, smothering me. Already I feel as if I need to walk with a stick; and even walking is difficult. But I have to walk away, even if I walk away limping.

And yet somehow I like this violence. The violation of my space so that I cannot write. The violence in those around me. The violence that I think I can put into words. Words come into my head, words made for a book. Banquo's murder ... a stab wound ... "let it come down".

XXII

The island lay about half a kilometre from the coast near Casablanca. It was not really in the Atlantic Ocean, but lay in a small estuary just off the coast beyond the city. It was in shallow water, and one could only get there by wading across the sandbank at low tide, and even then the water reached up to a person's waist.

Paul and Belquassim caught the train from Tangier to Casablanca on a windy Saturday morning. Belquassim had not been to the island, Paul had been there only once before, with Mohammed. Mohammed ... Belquassim thought. He has already taken Mohammed to this island that he loves so much. The train station in Casablanca was empty. A brown and white cat sat in the sun under the sign that announced, "Casablanca".

"It's a city of refugees," Paul had said. Belquassim stood under the sign and Paul took his photograph. Then another, one without Belquassim in it, just the sign. "Casablanca" – a bleak and empty sign. They had paid a taxi driver to take them to the estuary, and there an old man helped carry their bags across the small stretch of water. The water felt cold against Belquassim's thighs as he waded out, following Paul and the old man. As he looked across to the small piece of land Belquassim noticed the lush vegetation, with an occasional cypress tree looming above the fertile greenery. Birds and insects flitted from a tree to a bush and back again. The sounds soared up into the sky, blown by the air currents. Only the house where they were to stay was stationary, silent and deserted.

The house, the only building on the island, was ramshackle. It seemed not to have been maintained for many years. A wealthy Englishman owned it, and now he rented it to Paul. He had long ago abandoned the idea of a solitary existence far from London's streets with their moving snakes of people. There was no electricity or running water, so Paul had had to hire workers from the city to bring water, fresh food and candles. Belquassim did not know how long they were to stay on the island. For Paul it was a place to write, so he knew that they would stay as long as the writing continued. Every day, early in the morning as the sun rose high over the Casablanca skyline, Paul would grind some coffee beans in the small hand-held grinder and make himself a strong cup of coffee. Then he would take his typewriter up the hill and sit at a rickety desk under the olive trees, and write until lunchtime. Then he would come back to the house and make himself a sandwich of goat's cheese and olive oil. In the afternoons he would go for long solitary walks. He did not want Belquassim to accompany him on these walks, he preferred to walk alone. It was if Belquassim was not with him on the island. Paul was alone.

Belquassim walked, read the books of poetry that Paul had given him, and looked at nature. He loved the island and its beauty, but he was also filled with a despair that he had not known before as he saw Paul build an insuperable barrier around himself. For days they would not speak, and at night Paul would hold him in the dark, but it was as if he held his own body, felt his own skin. He showed no interest in Belquassim. A kind of nihilism set in, Paul eating, smoking hash and writing, and Belquassim reading. He read the poetry that they had read together, Keats, Shelley and Byron … Fitzgerald … romance, hope and beauty – he found them in the words on the pages of the dog-eared books that Paul had given him – what seemed to be so long ago, but in fact was only a few months. The writing that Paul had taught him to see, to touch and to feel.

Then Mohammed and a woman arrived. Paul had not told Belquassim that he expected Mohammed, but he must have made the plan a while before, as the island had no telephone with which to communicate with anyone outside it. Or maybe Paul had given a letter for Mohammed to one of the men who brought the water and he had posted it in Casablanca.

Belquassim watched the slim strong body, followed by the woman, wading out over the sand. Mohammed carried a small suitcase in one hand, and with the other he helped the woman. His face was as hard and beautiful as Belquassim remembered it. His eyes were the eyes of a statue and his mouth, although it smiled, held no promises. On the first night, over hashish and whisky he told Belquassim and Paul that the woman was his fiancée and the marriage date was set for later in the year. But Belquassim did not believe this: the woman was not young, and she was coarse. She did not wear the *haik*, but instead one of Mohammed's long shirts, as it was hot on the island. And when she moved he could see the scars of childbirth on her hips and stomach.

Belquassim had watched the relationship between Mohammed and Paul develop, first in Tangier, then in Fes and now on the island. He did not intervene. He knew that the relationship would eventually run its course, when the story was finished, when a book was born and when Mohammed, tired of hustling Paul, would move on to someone else. But as he watched, and as he moved around this picture of Paul and Mohammed, his eyes saw a story of uncertainty. What was his role in this story?

"Mohammed," Paul said, "knows the value of life." And, thought Belquassim, what do I know, if I do not know the value of life? During the day Mohammed would sit with Paul and tell him about his life. And Paul would either write down what he was saying, or tape the conversations on the small tape recorder that crackled when replayed. Belquassim would sit and listen to these stories. They were similar to those that he had told Paul himself, but he felt that they lacked the beauty that he had put into his own words. They lacked some essential feeling that he felt only he could capture. They were hard stories, without simplicity, but maybe Paul needed this now. Maybe he did not need beauty, maybe he needed to capture the strange morality of Mohammed's world so that he could measure his own world against it. Belquassim knew that, for now, Paul was far away, but he knew, he knew for certain, he would come back, back to their shared experiences, back to their common understanding, back to Jane. He just had to wait, and hope. But Paul did not believe in hope, he had told him this before.

"Hope!" he would laugh. "Hope in what, humanity? It is such a false emotion, hope. Hope is more false even than love, for hope allows a person to believe that he will ultimately attain something better. But he never will, and they never do."

They were sitting on the long curved terrace that surrounded the house. It was a cool evening. A breeze occasionally blew in off the milky water. From under the vine that curled above them on the stick-like poles Belquassim could see the first star, the evening star. It seemed to be alone in the firmament, but he knew it would not be alone for long, others would soon join it. "My life," Mohammed took a long drag on the hashish pipe, and leaned forward to hand his coffee cup to the woman: "Some more ..." He spoke the somnambulant whisper of the dead: "Some more, and give some more to Paul too." He handed the pipe to Belquassim who passed it on to Paul. Paul turned on the tape recorder. "Now you want to hear about my life. I have told you all the nice Moroccan stories, the belief of my people that goes with the music, those fantasies that the Nazarenes want to hear. Now do you want to write the real thing. That fucked-up real part that is my life story."

"Say it any way you want to," said Paul. "Before it gets printed I will read it to you, and you can tell me what you want to keep in and what you want to take out."

Mohammed smiled, "I was brought up in the Rif valley, the valley where once a man could grow olives and corn and survive. But with the French, things became different. They took the fertile land away from us. Oh, they were not as bad as they were in Algeria – there they just took it and killed the farmers – here in Morocco at least they paid us for the land. But payments, how long do they last? They called it a Protectorate, not a colony. But who did we need protection from? Only from them. Then one day we left the Rif. My father had died and my mother could no longer keep all the children fed. I am glad that he died, the bastard with his thick black moustache and hairy hands. He would beat my mother and then he would beat us. He was a mean man, my father, he would scream at my mother and then fuck her. We watched this, all of us children, the house was too small to hide anything. It became a custom in our lives, a bit like going to a picture show that you have seen before. My father would take off his belt – I can see it now in front of me, it had a heavy buckle, he said he had got it when he was in the Spanish army – and then he would whip my mother; across her breasts, on her face, and then he would fuck her, on the floor in the kitchen. The floor would be covered with her blood and sweat, and he would roll in it grunting all the while, saying over and over, "bitch, bitch, bitch". He died, a Spanish soldier killed him, somewhere I don't know where, the International Zone, Tangier seemed the best place to go to. Eventually neither my sister nor my mother could stand it either, Tangier that is, so they left for Fes – you know that part, you have visited them there, but I digress, that is another story. Me, I still go to Tangier. I love Tangier."

Mohammed took the coffee from the woman and sipped from the glass. "There is no sugar in it," he said. "Can't you remember that I take lots of sugar? If you want to be my wife these are things that you must remember." He reached out and pulled her to him, lifted her shirt, his shirt really, and looked at her. "But you do have something that I want even if you forget the sugar." His hand slid under the shirt. "Yes," he continued, "it's sweet and wet and smooth." The woman did not reply, but her eyes said, Take it if you want to. I want you to take it.

"We walked from the mountains to the city," Mohammed continued, "The road to Tangier was filled with people doing much like us. Donkeys piled up with goods, whole families driven out of their lives by famine. And we knew there was bread in the city, little bread, but bread anyway. All along the road were dead animals, cows and goats and donkeys. People could not afford to feed them, so they just left them to die when they could go no further. Crows sat on the dead flesh, pecking out the eyes of those that were newly dead. The eye is a delicacy and anyway the dead can no longer see. Or the crows would sit in the stomachs of those that had been there for a while, eating the bloody entrails. Occasionally we would see small children being picked clean by the same crows. They say the crows that developed a taste for the flesh of children never wanted to eat anything else again, so they died. I don't know, there still seem to be many crows on that road. We would hold a piece of mint to our noses as we passed, the smell could choke a man. Pus and blood oozed out from everywhere. If someone died on the road, we would just bury him then and there. It is the custom to bury a man within a day of his death, and so we buried them along the way. If you drive that road you will see hillock after hillock that is the dead. I buried two of my brothers on that road. One was only four years old, he could not survive on nothing. The other was killed in a fight – he had tried to steal from other travellers. I don't know if it was bread or hashish that he tried to steal. We did not get it anyway."

Mohamed took another drag on the pipe and breathed out the smoke, long and languid. "Remember when I first saw you, Paul. It was you and your woman on the terrace of that hotel – where was it again? – near the beach. You do not remember me from that day, but your woman, she will remember because she spoke to me. You did not speak. You sat still as you sit now. You do not talk. She looked at me, I thought she wanted to fuck me, but all she said was 'You must have big lungs to hold in so much smoke?' Where is she now? Why have you left her behind in Tangier? You know the city as well as I do. Maybe she will do something there, something that you do not like, ha." Mohammed laughed.

Paul turned the tape in the recording device over. "Go on with your life," he said quietly. Belquassim knew he did not want to speak about Jane. "I have a hatred of her illness, it stops her from being alive," he had said when Belquassim tried to raise his concerns. "And anyway I am alone now. Sentiment and memory cannot affect me. I put those feelings somewhere else, otherwise I cannot work."

"Click." The tape recorder started to record. Mohammed continued, "In her short life my mother gave birth to thirteen children. Thirteen! It's an unlucky number, so some of them had to die. Well, she lost two of us on that journey, and three others died later. They said it was tuberculosis, but it was a gangrenous misery that killed them. When we got to the city I could see that I would have to become a hustler, to feed my family and myself. Hustling for me is now a way of life, hustling the tourists. But I can also play music, so I hustle by night and play beautiful music in the *souk* by day. And we ate. I did not see all the bread that I had been promised, or that I had promised my mother – in that Eden also there was so little – but at least it was not a hunger that killed."

"My first fuck in the city ..." Mohammed's tone became lugubrious. "It was not really a fuck. I just saw a man hanging around the *Petit Souk*. He was standing outside one of the brothels. I was only fourteen but I knew about the brothels by then. One of my sisters worked in one. I sidled up to him and said, 'Why don't you go in, nice girls in there, nice clean girls. You won't get a sickness from them.' He just looked at me and answered, 'Brown boy, you look better than the girls, I like it young, the younger the better. Come.' And I followed him down the street. Under a doorway in the shade of the old woman's house – she used to give me bread when I was hungry – I sucked his cock. He was not circumcised and he smelled bad. And then he gave me fifty pesetas. That was what my mouth was worth then, fifty pesetas. It's worth a lot more today, I can tell you," and Mohammed laughed again. "That day, I had a new profession to choose from. Now I could be a thief and a whore. And after all, what is a whore, what is a thief? Just jobs like any other. The only time that I really hated it, the whoring I mean, was one night – near the beach I met an Englishman. He told me he was a playwright from London and that he wanted some fun. I followed him to his car, it was big and the windows were shadowed. Inside were three Spanish boys and a black. The Englishman said we were going to a party. A party for me promised more than just money, there would be food and whisky as well as sex. At the house I ate a whole chicken – I remember that I ate the whole oily bird and then I stuffed another one into my bag to take home. The Spanish boys were already undressing as I ate. I just watched them. Then three other Englishmen came in. One of them was holding a riding crop and his shirt had blood on it. One of the Spanish boys just bent over the bed and was fucked by the Englishman. The black took pictures. I could not do it that night – it reminded me of my father fucking my mother and me screaming. The Spanish boys were all screaming and whimpering. 'You fuckers,' I told the Spanish boys, 'don't you know your pictures are going to be sold and masturbated over in every European city? Is this what it is about?' I have muscles and big arms. 'Fuck you all!' I said, and hit the black. He came towards me with a knife until I grabbed one of the Englishmen. I held him against my chest and threatened to break his windpipe if the black came closer. Then I dragged the Englishman outside and beat him. To teach him a lesson: 'Don't fuck with weak boys, I might be young but I am also strong.' And then I took his money and ran off into the night. I left him there, I remember he said his name was Joe. As I took his money he laughed and said, 'Pretty boy, you will be back'. I found a lot of money in his wallet. Did I go back? Maybe ..."

"A few weeks later I met a Spanish couple. They were walking through the *souk* when I saw them. She was pretending to buy jewellery, but I knew that was not all she wanted. The man with her was grey and skinny and probably impotent. We had a meal together and they invited me back to their apartment. I fucked them both for a week or so, until I got bored. Bored with having to listen to her read me her shit poetry and bored with his begging for more. They said they thought of me as their son, but I was not their son and so I left. I am only my mother's son, and even of that sometimes I am not sure."

"And of course now you are writing my story. And you will print my story and take me to New York? You will take me to America, Paul, yes. But now, enough for today. I must eat, and tomorrow we will finish and I will go back home."

Supper that night was quiet, there was nothing more to say, Mohammed's words had numbed them all.

Paul drank a lot of the red wine that night. "I don't know if anyone ever tells the truth any more," he said to Belquassim when they were at last alone at the long silent table. "I never tell the truth and I don't expect anyone else to. I don't lie, I just don't say anything. Maybe that's the same as a lie, the omission. But I do know that once you reveal everything to another you fall under his power. If I ever told you one important thing this is it – don't reveal yourself completely to another." Paul looked outwards, as if for a moment he had to think about these words and give them a context. He went on: "Look what truth-telling did for Jane, look what truth-telling did for her." For the first time in weeks he leaned over and kissed Belquassim on the cheek. He looked at Belquassim, then, as if to explain the kiss, he said, "On the other hand, in Mohammed's case there is little difference between life and the narrative. Both are performances, and Mohammed performs well."

It must have been past midnight before they left the supper table and went to bed. Belquassim blew out the candle that stood on the low table next to the bed. There was no light at all, the moon had disappeared and the stars had followed her. He put out his hand to search for Paul in the dark. Paul wore no shirt and he felt the soft white flesh under his fingertips. He caressed the skin, moving his hands gently. "Why can't I let go?" Belquassim thought he heard Paul whisper in the dark, but he could not be sure. What could Paul not let go of, he wondered, hoping that it was himself. Maybe it was, but then maybe it was only the sound of the wind murmuring in the trees outside. Belquassim moved his fingers lightly over Paul's skin, bright diamonds appeared in front of his eyes and then they slept, so close it seemed as if they were one person. But Belquassim knew, though he could not think this, that they were two people.

The next day Mohammed and the woman left the island. Mohammed left behind the tapes of his stories, and Paul transcribed them under the olive tree. Many years later Belquassim was to learn that, after a book of Mohammed's stories had been published – the words written by Paul, Mohammed did go to

New York. But he quickly came back – he hated it. In New York he was not in control of his life. New York was full of stories that he did not know, or could not comprehend. So he had left, come back to the familiar amorality of Tangier, and talked to whoever would listen to him.

XXIII

I feel terrible today. My whole body shakes, my hands are sweating and my migraine makes me see circles of light every time I close my eyes. Every time Cherifa tries to touch me I push her away. It is not that I do not want her, it's just that to feel her, feel her fingers in my hair … it is foreign, it burns my skin, and her touch is rough and hard. I want Paul. I just want him to read his stories to me. I just want to hear that voice. I just want to hear him speak his words, those desperate words. I want to feel his fingers that now feel only a pen. I want to hear our story. And my leg, that leg that keeps straight and stiff when I walk – it has always been a badge of pride, I am a survivor – now it is painful. It is so painful.

No-one here understands how I panic, but they all give advice. Paul has been adamant – I should look for some kind of anxiety medication when I am in New York, but I have never done this. Belquassim told me that I should eat special herbs when I feel my heart beat and I cannot breathe. He even gave me some crushed green leaves to mix in with coffee. Allen, who is in Tangier at the moment, told me to breathe in deeply. "Breathe in different colours," he said to me the other day. "Deep blue and emerald green helps to bring about a calmness. Red, don't breathe in red. That colour is too strong." Allen is with Bill, and so Bill with his pills is not around that much any more. Allen now takes up all his time, the time he is awake, that is. And apparently Jack is coming in from Paris, then Bill will never come here. Strange, even Bill, the autonomous independent Bill, who thinks only of his drugs and his needles, needs people. Look how he needs Allen when he is here. It is almost as if he cannot let him out of his sight as then he may just disappear.

I wish Paul would come back here. I wish I could die.

Oh God, please don't let me die. Don't let me die. I am sorry, so sorry.

There is something wrong today. I cannot put my finger on it. Maybe it is the weather, or maybe it is the paragraph that I have just written for my book. Where these words will go I do not know. But the words have beaten me. They have beaten even me – I the untouchable have been moved by my own words. But do I care? No, it's just the beauty of it that moves me, beauty always does. But it moves me for such a short time. It only moves me when I am reading it, then it goes – this feeling.

"Amar was running after the car. It was still there, ahead of him, going further away and faster. He could never catch it, but he ran because there was nothing else to do. And as he ran, his sandals made a terrible flapping noise on the hard surface of the highway, and he kicked them off, and ran silently and with freedom. Now for a moment he had the exultant feeling of flying along the road behind the car. It would surely stop. He could see the two heads in the window's rectangle, and it seemed to him that they were looking back. The car had reached a curve in the road; it passed out of sight. He ran on. When he got to the curve the road was empty."

Betrayal! The road is always empty, no matter how quickly we run, no matter how we search. It can only be empty. And there is really nothing that I can do about this, except put it into words, words ever more beautiful – words more beautiful than I can comprehend or articulate. In any event, what is there to search for? Nothing really, or at least nothing that makes me care enough. I do not mind if the road stays empty for I am empty.

XXIV

It was morning, a misty morning, the mist sitting daintily on the roof of the old house. Paul had already made and drunk his coffee. He was now far on the other side of the island writing. Belquassim sat on the veranda. He was writing too. In his notebook he tried to capture what his life was like with Paul and Jane. He also sometimes copied poems into the book, ones that he wanted some day to read to someone else, the poems that he wanted to remember. He had just finished writing about Mohammed's visit, his reaction to the sexual languidness, the hint of menace, in Mohammed's relationship with Paul. It was not jealousy that he wrote about, rather it was confusion. His emotions sometimes ran loose, sometimes he could not control his feelings of exclusion. He held the pencil tightly in his right hand, between thumb and forefinger, and copied out lines from a poem in an anthology that Jane had given him for her birthday. She always gave gifts on her birthday. "Birthdays are for celebrating," she once told him, "celebrating because after every birthday we are coming closer and closer to death, so we must celebrate on a birthday. We must celebrate others, not ourselves." It was a poem by Dante, a poem about celebrating love. He had just finished copying the last verse into his diary.

> *And I wish we all did nothing but talk about love*
> *and I wish that they were just as glad to be there*
> *As I believe the three of us would be.*

Belquassim read the words out loud: "*And I wish we all did nothing but talk about love.*" He moved his chair out of the sun and into the shadow that was cast by the heavy vine leaves. It was hot in the sun. He looked up, and saw a man coming rapidly across the sandbank. Belquassim did not recognise him, he was so far away. Then he stepped out of the water and onto the dry island, and Belquassim saw that it was one of the men who brought them food and water. He hurried over with a piece of paper in his hand, and gave it to Belquassim.

"It's for the Nazarene," he said. He was panting, he must have run some of the way.

"Thanks, I will give it to him," answered Belquassim.

"No, you must give it now," the man replied, "it is urgent. The post office said that it was an urgent telegram from Tangier and that it has already been delayed on the way." Belquassim picked up the orange envelope and saw Paul's name handwritten on the outside. That must be the postmaster's handwriting if it was a telegram.

"Thanks," he said to the messenger. He went inside to get some money. Paul always left his wallet on the table in the dining room. "Take whatever you need from it," he had told Belquassim. "I only need money for food while I am here, so take what you want."

Belquassim took the envelope and walked quickly across the island to where he knew Paul would be sitting. He always sat in the same spot under the olive tree. As he walked he hummed a tune. He tried to put Dante's words to this old Moroccan song. They seemed to fit quite well, he thought, as he sang the first two lines again. Paul looked up as he saw Belquassim. He did not greet him, he continued typing. "Click click click" went his fingers. "I'm sorry," said Belquassim quietly, "I know you don't like to see me before lunchtime, but this came for you. The man who brought it said that it was urgent, I don't know if it is, but I thought I should bring it anyway." Paul stretched out his hand and took the envelope. Without looking at it he slid it under the typewriter on the rickety table. He said nothing. Belquassim turned and walked back to the house. There was nothing more to do, he had given the telegram to Paul.

A little later, near lunchtime Paul came back to the house. Belquassim had turned on the radio and was listening to the news.

It was in Arabic and was about the progress of the talks between the Moroccan king and the French. I wonder what will happen when we are left to ourselves, he thought, when I am left to myself. Paul had still not read the telegram. He poured himself a glass of hot red wine and tore at the orange corners of the glued up envelope. The telegram was short, only one line. It read, "*Return now Jane seriously ill*". It was dated three days before. There was no signature or the name of who had sent it. Paul looked at the writing, from the expression on his face it looked to Belquassim as if he was thinking of something else, it was if someone else was reading the same telegram. He drank the glass of wine and said, "We have to go, now. Let's get our things. We can send for the rest of whatever is here some other time." One hour later they were at the station in Casablanca, and in the evening they were in Tangier.

They hurried from the station to the house in the *Petit Socco*. It was raining. The wind beat at their bodies as it howled across the sea and up the streets, and the rain sank into their light clothing. The streets were deserted. The house was dark, none of the lamps were lit. The dust moved under their feet as they entered. There was no-one there. Paul took the telegram from the pocket of his jacket, the paper was wet as the rain had seeped through his shirt. It was a summer shirt, an island shirt, it just covered his skin rather than protected him from the elements. The telegram said nothing. "She can only be at Cherifa's," Paul said, "there is no-one else here who she would want to be with. Show me where she lives, I can't remember the house, especially in this weather, and it is getting dark."

"We must put on dry clothes and take our raincoats before we go," Belquassim replied, "we are soaked."

"No," Paul said, "we must go now. Hurry and show me the house." Belquassim shivered. The urgency in Paul's voice ripped into his chest. He took the keys of the house from Paul and led him down the stairs and into the street. He would have to show Paul the way; he would, once again, have to lead Paul through the city.

Cherifa lived on the other side of the *Grand Socco*. It was not very far away, but to Belquassim the journey seemed endless. They walked in silence. Belquassim did not speak, he was not brave enough to say what he was thinking. And he was thinking, that he knew that Jane was not at Cherifa's house. Oh, *Allah*, what if, *Allah*, what if ...? The words in his head sounded over and over. When they came to the narrow building where Cherifa lived with some of the other women from the market a sour smell seemed to creep up their nostrils. The house was lit and there was the sound of Moghrebi voices inside. Belquassim knocked on the door. It was not a big house but at least two families, including Cherifa and her women, lived there. He called to the market woman in Moghrebi. The drumming of the rain continued, but now he was not sure if the sound was the sounds of rain on the roof of the house or if it was the heartbeat in his head. He called out again. Then Paul also called out. "Quiet," said Belquassim, "they will not come down if they hear the voice of a Nazarene." He could see Paul's hands shaking, he was not sure if it was the cold or his fear.

Belquassim reached over and took Paul's hand as if to warm it, but Paul pulled it away. "Call again," he said. Belquassim called out again, this time louder. After a few minutes someone leaned out over the balcony.

"What is it, who do you want?" Belquassim could not see who was speaking. He asked for Cherifa. A few minutes later the door was opened and Cherifa stood there. She looked huge, silhouetted against the background of the lamps. Before they could say anything she said, "She is not here, she was too sick so we took her to the hospital and the doctor."

Paul looked at her, his eyes glazed over with a look of hatred that Belquassim had never seen before. "Which hospital, where is it?" he asked.

"The one with the nuns in it, opposite the Cinema Paris on the Rue de Fes," Cherifa replied. As she did so Belquassim thought he saw a tear run down her rough brown cheek but he could not be certain. Her voice did not betray her emotions, it was cold.

All Paul said was, "We have to get a taxi. It is too far to walk there."

They hurried from the street towards the Avenue Hassan. There were no taxis to be seen. The rain came down with greater ferocity. Belquassim went into a bar just ahead of them to telephone for a taxi. A man, overhearing his request to the barman, offered to be their taxi. When Belquassim told him where they wanted to go to he laughed and asked an exorbitant price for the journey, much more than a taxi would have cost, but Belquassim accepted the offer anyway. He knew that in this weather and at this time a taxi would have taken hours to get to the bar. The car was parked a few metres from where Paul stood outside. His hair was soaking wet, water dripped into his eyes and down his face, and occasionally he wiped the water away with his hand across his mouth.

The journey seemed to take hours when in fact it probably took only twenty minutes. At the hospital Paul paid the driver who grinned evilly. They went inside the opaque white building. A nurse stood at the reception desk, dressed in white, the traditional habit of the Sisters of Mercy. She looked at the two of them as they entered and frowned, Belquassim could see that to her they looked like villains or thieves, both dripping wet with only their island clothing for covering. "Jane Bowles," Paul said, "where is she?"

"And who may you be?" the nun replied. She wrinkled her nose as if there was a bad smell in the air. There probably was, thought Belquassim, the smell of despair.

"My wife, she is my wife," said Paul and moved towards the nun. He was shaking terribly now, his teeth making a ringing sound in the silent antiseptic air.

"Oh, Mr Bowles, yes we have been expecting you for some days now. Your wife has been asking for you. She is upstairs in one of the single wards. The doctor has just been in to see her. If you like I will ask her to wait and you can speak to her after you have seen your wife. But now I must get you something else to put on, you cannot go into the ward in those clothes, you are soaking wet."

Paul gripped her by the shoulders, "Let me just go in. I will take these clothes off later. Just let me go in."

"No," the nun insisted. "Come with me." She led them down a corridor and into a small room where she gave Paul a pair of white trousers and a white shirt. "Put these on," she said. Paul stripped off his clothing and put on the garments. Belquassim remained in the clothes he had arrived in. He was an outsider here. Even the nun assumed that he would not go into the ward, there he had no place. They followed her up some stairs and down a long corridor. Belquassim felt as if he were the devil, a devil that had invaded this convent.

At the end of a corridor was a small altar with a statue of a woman on it. Belquassim who had never been into a Catholic church felt the eyes of the holy mother pass over him. Was her smile compassionate, and was her compassion meant for him? Her blue robes shimmered in the candlelight, and incense wove through the air around her. For a reason which he could not express, the odour of the incense and her white porcelain face comforted him.

The nun pointed to a door, Paul went inside, and Belquassim waited outside in the corridor. The door was open and he could see a small figure in the bed. Paul leaned over the bed, and then sank to his knees. He put out his hand and touched Jane's face, he took her hand and held it to his cheek, but there was no sound, no movement, just the sound of her breathing. Her breath was even, there was no movement to break the silence. Belquassim could hear Paul's voice murmuring in the distance, but not what he said, only that it was tender and warm. He gave Jane his words. Belquassim waited and watched for a long time. He leaned against the wall and watched them in their intimacy. He had never been so close to something like this before and he felt awed. Whatever it was, he felt its intensity rush over him, clouding his thoughts as he battled to comprehend it. Why her, he thought, why her?

It seemed an eternity before he heard footsteps behind him. A woman with a stethoscope around her neck approached the door. She walked in and touched Paul on the shoulder. He started, interrupted, his space displaced. She beckoned to him and he followed her outside and into the corridor. They stood near Belquassim and spoke. "Your wife has had a stroke," the doctor said. "I do not know what brought it on in such a young woman, but because she is young it may not have affected her as badly as it would an older person. But we cannot really tell the extent of the damage yet. I think she will be unable to see properly and her memory for things like words may have gone. But I cannot be certain."

"What must I do?" said Paul. His hand still shook as he took her by the shoulders. "What can I do?"

"You can only wait," the doctor replied. "At the moment she has been given sedatives, but when she awakes, which will be some time in the morning, you must be here for her." Her tone was judgmental. Paul, who had tried never to judge anyone and was not concerned about the judgement of others, seemed to shrink into the white wall. He had never seemed so small to Belquassim, he had always been strong, now he shrank. "Maybe," the doctor continued, "– and of this I am not sure – you should take her to Spain. I do not know at this point whether you will need to, but I will give you my advice a bit later when things are more stable."

"Thank you. I will come back early tomorrow morning," said Paul. Belquassim wondered what he was thanking her for. She had given him nothing, but it was as if he was a child now. Maybe now he would need someone to take care of him.

Outside the hospital they found a taxi. It was an old converted ambulance. The driver told them that he had bought it from the hospital when they had brought in the newer, more equipped ambulances. In the car Paul was silent. Belquassim did not speak. There was nothing left to say.

At the house in the *Petit Socco* Paul went up the stairs. First he went into the area where they would often have their suppers, especially if the evening was a little cool. Jane was a good cook and she would often experiment with new meals. They were nice. He sat at the long table. Then he reached up to the noticeboard that was above the table and took down the photograph Jane had pinned up some time before, the picture of the two of them on the beach at Rabat, the picture in which

Paul held her book on his knees. He then got up and went to what they had always cheerfully called "Jane's cupboard", where he found a bottle of whisky, and poured himself a glass. It was as if Belquassim had seen this before. It was a replay, only the character was different. He remembered the yellow glow of the liquid that Jane would pour languidly into her glass. Now Paul poured the whisky. He even used the glass that was Jane's favourite, it had fluted sides. He sat at the table for a long time, not speaking. Belquassim thought he could see the images running around in his head, but he could not understand them, they were not words. The photograph from the noticeboard seemed to leer out at Belquassim although it was no longer there. It seemed to speak to him, I am here, it said. He noticed the small newspaper cutting that was still pinned to the board and remembered what he had loved about her and what he had eventually come to hate. He hated her now. She was not like Mohammed, someone who could come between Paul and himself for a moment, a tangible moment that would be over either today or tomorrow or maybe even the next day. She was always there, Paul would never leave her. And no love for Paul by anyone else could ever break that bond.

Much later they went to bed. Paul lay next to him, not sleeping. He just lay in the dark wrapped up in his silent desires, and these desires did not include Belquassim or anything that he could ever give to him.

In the morning they got up. Belquassim made the coffee while Paul dressed. The liquid was strong and black. The rain was still pelting down, it was unending, it was unnerving. They drank and then Belquassim went to look for a taxi. On the way down to the main street he saw Cherifa. She did not look at him, it was as if they had never known one another. A small boy came up to him while he stood on the corner looking for a taxi. The boy gave him a letter. "Message from Cherifa," he said. "She said to tell you that you must tell Jane that she is waiting for her to come back, and to give her the letter because it says that she loves Jane." Cherifa did not know that Jane could no longer see to read the letter. Cherifa did not know that Jane probably no longer knew how to read, had probably forgotten the words.

"I will take it," he said. "Tell Cherifa to visit Jane in the hospital, she needs her." But he knew Cherifa never would visit Jane. He looked around but the market woman was gone. Maybe she knew that now there was no alternative to her life, or maybe she just had things she needed to do. He found a taxi and directed it to the house.

Paul had still not spoken. As he got into the taxi he said to Belquassim, "I have managed in my life to control everything. I have remained detached. I am indifferent. But I can't remain indifferent to this. Forgive me, I cannot explain it any longer, I don't even know if I want to try and explain it because then it will become real. Forgive me." He covered his face in his hands. There were no tears. The taxi cruised slowly down the road past the beach. Belquassim looked out and saw the Hotel Mirador, its doors were shut, and he thought about Jane's brown eyes looking into his as he sat with the young boys, his back against the wall, hoping and waiting, hoping for something more.

At the hospital Belquassim once again followed Paul up the stairs to the door of her room. The Madonna in the corner was still there. She looked up and forgave him for all his thoughts. He wanted to confess them to her but he knew that he could not. He longed to reach out and touch her soft comforting blue robes but he knew in his heart that they would be cold and hard, she was made of plaster. Her eyes followed him as he sat on his haunches against the wall of the room. Waiting.

Five days later Paul accompanied Jane to Malaga in Spain. The doctor had said that she would get better treatment in Spain, there was nothing more that they could do for her in Tangier. Jane could no longer speak, she could no longer see. All she could do was feel the touch of Paul's hands stroking her hair, her arms, and down her back.

XXV

Once again I am indifferent to everything around me. It escaped me for a moment, this great indifference, but only for a moment. Now it has returned.

I do not care enough to be sad. I do not care enough to be angry. My life in Tangier will go on. I am the outsider here. I am now alone.

XXVI

Belquassim finished the last drop of the yellow liquid, it burnt in his throat. He raised his arm, as Jane had done so many times, and beckoned the barman for another. The yellow sparkled in the half-light, it glinted as it moved in the glass. To both of them, he again whispered silently.

He looked out of the long windows and saw Spain in the distance The European coast was only twenty-five kilometres away. It was another world. Maybe if he strained his eyes he could see Jane's grave. He knew that she had been buried in Malaga. He had received a telegram from Paul, which he still kept in the bottom drawer of a cupboard at home. It said, "*Jane died yesterday. I think I will bury her where she can see the sea and, if she looks hard enough, she will see Tangier. P.B.*" Once, when a friend of his planned to escape Morocco by crossing the straits to Spain, Belquassim had asked him to visit the cemetery at Malaga and to send him a letter describing the grave. His friend had never done this favour for him. Maybe, as was the case with many refugees, he had never reached Spain.

A slight sound of movement at the back entrance to the bar caught his attention above the music and the laugh of the woman. He looked across to the doorway – it was the one that was not often used, the door through which only those who knew the city well would enter. The boy who stood there looked across at him. He looked as if he had been sent to the bar to find someone. He was about twelve – but these days one could never be sure of a boy's age – not old enough to shave, but old enough to fuck. His eyes betrayed his emotions: they were dark and care showed in them. But no, he is not yet old enough, thought Belquassim, he cannot be old enough to sell himself. And when I sold myself, what did I receive in payment? Only a dream, and I have already spent my dream. He put his hand to his shoulder and felt the small raised scar on his skin, it nestled between his shoulder blades, protected.

The boy smiled at Belquassim and came across the floor to the long counter that ran alongside the window. He reached out and took Belquassim's hand. As he did so he said quietly, "Come Papa, supper will soon be ready and Mamma is waiting for us, so that we can eat. Tonight she has cooked my favourite, a lamb tagine with couscous. Come, let's go home."

Belquassim drained the rest of the whisky from his glass. It ran like a flame down his throat. He got up slowly from the barstool and took the boy's hand. Gently the boy led him across the bar towards the door, the front door that led down to the ocean. In a hoarse voice he replied, "Yes, let us go home."

Acknowledgements

In the course of writing this novel many writers have been close to me. I may have used their words: a phrase, a sentence, a paragraph, some poetry. Readers of this book will know these words or sentences or paragraphs or poetry; they will know who wrote them. They will also know why they are placed where they are in my text. I am grateful to all those who are dead and who have inspired me to love words.

More especially I am indebted to Paul Bowles, Jane Bowles, Mohammed Choukri, Mohammed Mrabet, William Burroughs, Allen Ginsberg, Truman Capote, Jean Genet, W.H. Auden, Gertrude Stein, Alice B. Toklas, Natalie Barney, Albert Camus, Jean Paul Sartre and others whose names are not here or who have been forgotten.

Printed in the United States
By Bookmasters